FRANK WOLF, SOLD SHORT

•

I watched their reflections in the chandelier—the killers in miniature, hundreds of them upside down and mirrored in the polished crystal as they climbed the staircase, guns drawn. They came to the head of the stairs, split like a forked tongue to flatten themselves against the ballroom walls. I lunged to my left and fired down at a slight angle, one, two, three shots into the first one before he could blink in disbelief.

At the same time, the second gunman opened up on me. His bullets hammered into the piano: wood splintering, steel strings snapping, flying, and twanging, the sound like crazy banjo music. I squeezed off three shots, which missed. He fired a second volley, *ploom, ploom, ploom,* the slugs punching holes in the boards where I lay. I fired the final shot from the .32—and missed him again. . . .

MARC DAVIS

DIRTY
MONEY

TO MY GOOD FRIEND,
ZACK NAUTH.
— KEEP ON
KEEPING ON!
LABOR NEEDS YOU,
Marc Davis

A DELL BOOK

Published by
Dell Publishing
a division of
Bantam Doubleday Dell Publishing Group, Inc.
666 Fifth Avenue
New York, New York 10103

Interior design by Jeremiah B. Lighter

ISBN: 0-440-21064-X

Printed in the United States of America

Published simultaneously in Canada

February 1992

10 9 8 7 6 5 4 3 2 1

RAD

Again, to my wife, Judy.
And to Kevin and Laura.

My sincere thanks to Philip G. Spitzer, extraordinary agent and gentleman; and to Jacqueline Cantor, wise and talented editor who saw further and deeper.

I also want to thank Harry McGinnis, formerly an officer and evidence technician with the Chicago Police Department, for the generous gift of his time and expertise.

Marc Davis

His face looked like a flower, the flesh unfolding like the petals of some deep, scarlet blossom. He had been a client of mine some years ago, but now I hardly recognized him. The bullet had entered the back of his head and exited through his nose, exploding the features of what was once a rather handsome man in his late forties.

I sailed the photograph back across Duffy's desk. He picked it up, still squinting at me over the top of his glasses.

"Yeah, I know him," I said. "Abel Nockerman. Nocky, they called him. Commodity trader. Very successful. Made a bundle in the market. He owned a brokerage firm in the Board of Trade building. I did some work for him a while back."

"You worked for the man?" Duffy asked. "Is that why your name's in his address book? What could a guy like you do for Nockerman?"

I heard the lilt of the old sod in Duffy's weary voice, the legacy of his County Mayo ancestors, tempered by the flat, brittle nasalities of Chicago's back-of-the-yards district. Lieutenant Patrick J. Duffy, Area One Homicide, Chicago Police Department. His plump face was suffused with a rosy tint. He smelled of lime after-shave lotion and Tullamore Dew.

His thinning red hair was turning gray, the collar of his blue oxford button-down was starting to fray, and his necktie was a little wider than what was fashionable this season. On the wall behind his head was an official photograph of the superintendent of police. Old Soupy was not smiling.

"About seven, eight years ago," I said, "Nockerman asked me to check out a guy he was planning to do some business with."

"Who was the guy and what kind of business?"

"I don't know about the business. The man's name was Mario Arcana. He owned a couple restaurants."

"Where does he live?" Duffy asked.

"Nowhere. He's dead."

"What did Nockerman want to know about him?"

"The usual. Who were his friends, his enemies, his business associates, credit history, if he had Outfit connections."

"Outfit connections? Why the hell would he want to know that?"

"Nockerman didn't want to do business with Mafia people," I said.

"So tell me, was Arcana connected?"

"No, he was just a heavy gambler. Dice, horses, commodities, whatever. Big loser for years, then suddenly he got lucky in the market after Nockerman became his broker."

"How'd Arcana die?"

"He was in a boat off the Florida coast. Washed overboard. Nockerman and another guy were with him. A coroner's jury said it was an accident."

"Was it?"

"Looked like it."

"I still don't understand something, Wolf," Duffy said. He leaned across his cluttered desk. "Nockerman's a guy could afford the best, right? So how come he hired you? I mean, he coulda gone to one of the big agencies, or to someone like Florentino, or the Berkstein Brothers."

I ignored the insult. I'd known Duffy since his earliest days on the force, and I liked him. He was a good cop, decent, not known to be kinky. Once in a while over the years we worked on the same case, he for the public, me for a client. One or two of these I cracked before he did, and he was embarrassed before his superiors. He didn't like getting edged by a P.I.

"Nockerman hired me because I knew him when we were kids in the old neighborhood," I said. "I lost track of him for a long time after he graduated high school. Then I started running into him now and then—the race track, Wrigley Field, a hockey game. He had made a lot of money by then. Ran with that LaSalle Street crowd. But once in a while he'd give me some work. Mostly odds and ends related to his brokerage business. I checked out a few employees, a few customers, routine stuff. Then he gave me this Arcana job, and that was the last time I worked for him. You want to fill me in on this thing?"

Duffy uttered a noisy sigh, closed his eyes briefly, slumped in his swivel chair with the chronic exhaustion of a middle-aged cop with half a lifetime of hard duty through every circle of this urban hell. He knew the vagaries of the human soul and its endless agonies as intimately as any priest.

"Nockerman was killed last week," he said.

I nodded my head. "Yeah, I saw it in the papers."

Duffy continued, reciting in a somnolent voice, "Single shot from a .45, execution style, extremely close range. The apartment wasn't ransacked and there was no sign of forced entry. But Nockerman's ex-wife thinks some money might have been taken. She says he kept a lot of cash on hand, sometimes a hundred grand or more. The doorman remembers nothing. He can't recall when Nockerman went in or out, or if he had any visitors. Very helpful fellow. Permanently stoned."

"Who discovered the body?" I asked.

"Nockerman's daughter. She had a key."

"Did she live with him?"

"No, she's got her own place."

"Is she a suspect?"

"No," Duffy said.

"Anything interesting in the autopsy?"

"No."

"You got any leads?"

"Nothing solid. Now, what do you know about Nockerman?"

"Not a hell of a lot," I said. "He gambled heavy, played the markets, ran with young women. No enemies, no Outfit trouble, no juice loans, no debts to bookmakers, and his brokerage firm was clean, far as I know."

Duffy's eyebrows lifted. "You checked out his company?"

"I got curious, so I looked. No complaints from the C.F.T.C., Illinois Consumer Fraud, or the Better Business Bureau."

"What's the C.F.T.C.?"

"Commodity Futures Trading Commission. Government agency like the S.E.C., for the futures market."

"I'll tell you what bothers me," Duffy said. "Why did Nockerman look for an Outfit tie-in with this Arcana guy?"

"I have no idea."

"Take a wild guess."

I shrugged. "Some things in life remain a mystery."

He fixed me with the icy stare of an inquisitor, eyes narrowed in disbelief. "What's the real story here, Wolf?" he asked. "Was Nocky a bad boy? Did you do something naughty for him? I look into this and find something, Wolf, I'll yank your fucking license."

"There's nothing to find, Lieutenant."

"I want to see your reports on the Arcana investigation."

"There are no reports. Nockerman didn't want anything on paper. I told him everything verbally."

Duffy chuckled ruefully. "You son of a bitch."

I looked pointedly at my watch, then glanced up at Duffy. "I got a ball game to catch."

"Yeah, go ahead," he said. "But look at this epidemic of stockbrokers murdered since Wall Street fell on its ass."

"The market's dangerous," I said. "Like playing with strangers in a no-limit card game."

"You figure a client of his did it?"

"Who knows? But I told you, Nocky wasn't a stockbroker. He was a commodity broker. There's a big difference."

"Yeah, yeah stocks, bonds, whatever. It's all the same hustle. You hear anything, Frank, phone me, huh?"

"Sure, Pat."

"You going to the Cubs–Pittsburgh game?"

"Yeah, want to come? I'll buy you a seat. Do you good to get out. Get some sunshine on your face."

"I'm working today, Frank. I just can't take off like you self-employed P.I.'s."

"Come on, we'll talk about the Nockerman case. Make it official police business."

"Good-bye, Frank."

"Try to get away for the second game. I'll be in the center-field bleachers. High up, under the scoreboard."

* * *

Poor Nocky. May he rest in peace. He had his faults and eccentricities, but I hated to see him that way. Looking at his picture, I had felt sick for an instant. But it passed. All these years in the business and I'm still not used to it. Maybe if I hadn't known him . . .

I remembered that day a few years ago when he had shown me around the Board of Trade. We stood together in the visitors' gallery, watching the action on the trading floor below.

"You can win or drop a million here, Frank. Just like that," Nocky had said, snapping his fingers to illustrate. He spoke in that strange basso voice of his, perpetually hoarse from overuse in the pits.

The tour guide commenced her prepared spiel. "Ladies and gentlemen, welcome to the Chicago Board of Trade, the world's largest commodity exchange. Over a million contracts are traded here daily in such commodities as wheat, corn, oats, soybeans, silver, government national mortgages . . ."

I stared down through the glass into the swarming mass of humanity congealed in clusters on the floor. Madness in the trading pits. They brayed like demented donkeys, waved their hands in semaphoric frenzy, slaves to their unrelenting mania—to buy, to sell, five thousand, fifty thousand, a half-million bushels in a single deal. The inmates of Bedlam might seem sane by comparison.

"Look at that riot," Nockerman said, chuckling. "Pack a lunatics, huh? I seen fights down there you wouldn't believe. Traders kickin' and punchin' each other out." Then he turned to me, laughing. "There's just one sure thing in life, Frank, human nature. Bet on it every time, you can't fuckin' lose."

"You understand what's going on down there?" I asked.

"This is my business, Frank. It's Vegas, but bigger and faster. I love it, it's a whole world in itself."

Yes, I thought, and a perfect symbol for the larger world beyond.

But Nockerman was always a shooter, even as a kid. He was one of my boyhood heroes, one of those fabulous urban Olympians of my youth who had some special ability I respected and admired.

Nocky's talent was his knack for making money, and for

attracting beautiful women. He usually had plenty of both. He was always involved in some lucrative hustle. In high school he ran an unlicensed, outlaw livery service, using his father's car to chauffeur his fellow students to and from football games and Saturday night dances. With the money he earned he bought closeouts and damaged goods, then turned them over for a tasty profit. I heard he made a small fortune. When he got older, his enterprises became more complex and venturesome, his women likewise.

I walked briskly down the street toward the parking lot to retrieve my car. Springtime in Chicago, the first Saturday in May. Derby day, in fact. The sun shone dimly through a smoky scrim, the air was heavy with humidity and noxious vapors, the city awash in the stench of its own vitality.

2

On my way to Wrigley Field a sudden wind came up, prelude to impending rain. Then it fell, straight down like beads of lead. I looked to every point of the compass for a break in the clouds, some fissure of light to mark the perimeter of the storm. Nothing. The rain would fall for hours. The Cubs–Pirates game would be called.

I went back to my office on Clark Street near Fullerton, a Spartan two-room suite on the second floor of a no-nonsense all-brick professional building, without ornament or distinction.

My outer door is steel, with a super-pickproof dead-bolt lock, reinforced with heavy-duty doorjambs. Nobody can break in unless they've got an oxyacetylene torch, or nitro.

The sign on the door says:

FRANK D. WOLF
LICENSED INVESTIGATOR

The anteroom was bare and unoccupied, except for a small steel desk and chair, and a chrome couch with brown vinyl cushions. Ten years in the business and I've never had a secretary, not even a temp. I write and type my own reports, and make my own phone calls.

The inner office is mine, a larger room with a pair of barred windows fronting the street. I had the bars installed several years ago to keep out the uninvited.

The furniture is simple, practical, inexpensive: a bank of black four-drawer filing cabinets, gray steel shelving for my tape-recording equipment, cameras, lenses, other odds and ends, a wooden bookcase for my phone directories, street guide crisscross, my handful of legal books. In the closet is a small fireproof safe with nothing in it. There are two chairs for clients and one for me, a very costly, very comfortable recliner of fleshy black leather. My large walnut desk is buried beneath layers of clutter.

Hidden under the desk on the right side is a snub-nose .32-caliber Smith & Wesson, conveniently at hand in a leather holster affixed to the wood. On the other side, also out of sight, is a toggle switch. It activates a simple, battery-operated device of my own invention. When I hit it with my knee—an act that presumably cannot be observed by visitors in my office—a light blinks on at the cash register at the deli on the corner. A pal of mine owns the place and when he or his designates see that light, they know to call the cops for help and give them my address. I've used it on several occasions to save my ass, but only after that first time when I had wished for something like it an instant before I was cold-cocked. When I eventually came to, an irreplaceable document had been taken from me, along with my irreplaceable sense of security. In that moment I was disabused of the notion that I was immune to calamity, a delusion common to so many of us, especially P.I.'s, cops, newspaper reporters, paramedics, emergency-room surgeons, and others involved peripherally in the disasters of their fellow creatures. Once you take that first serious, painful hit, the world seems a far nastier place.

For the rest of the day I did paperwork, writing a final report to a client, typing the story flat out from my notes on the old Underwood manual the way I once did when I worked general assignment for the *Chicago Daily Scrutinizer,* enjoying the sound and feel of that ancient black machine.

About four in the afternoon, I turned on the radio to catch the Derby. I had a heavy bet on the three-to-five favorite. Short odds, but money in the bank. The track band played "My Old Kentucky Home," and the horses were off. A little more than two minutes later a fifteen-to-one shot won the roses. My horse finished fourth. That's what I get for betting a sure thing.

I posted the loss in my mental ledger. I was down more than eight grand, year-to-date. But I wasn't worried. There's a symmetry to the universe and everything in it—all matter, all energy, all phenomena. You live long enough, the cosmic books will balance. Meanwhile, I owed a certain bookmaker five yards.

Somewhere in the endless gridwork of one-way streets south of Roosevelt Road in Cicero is an ancient red-brick three-flat building, one of countless others in a neighborhood cloned from the same design. But the top-floor apartment of this particular edifice was an Outfit gambling joint, its cramped chambers redolent with smoke and the funky sweat of losers. Not exactly Casino Royale, but most gamblers don't mind where they drop their dough as long as there's plenty of action. Blackjack and craps are the house games, and the small shabby living room is cluttered with tables and folding chairs, where the suckers hunch thoughtfully over their cards, absorbed in the serious work of their play. In the dining room there is a noisy crap game, the dealer chattering in a passionless monotone, the shooters loudly imploring their gods or demigods. By day the place is a wire room, and green chalkboards hang from the walls, with horses and odds from tracks around the country scrawled in between the ruled lines. They'll take your bet on almost anything that moves.

The joint has been here for more than a year, more than overdue for a hasty relocation elsewhere, a step ahead of the anticipated bust. The news always precedes the event; somebody calls and gives fair warning: the heat's coming down, pack it up and move it out.

Presiding over it all as host and manager is an Outfit factotum named Freedo. As I came in he welcomed me with a jolly thump on the back. "Frankie boy, how the hell are ya?" His face was a lunar landscape, gray, full of craters, the burnt-out pits of a once-volcanic acne. I gave him five crisp, new C notes. He stuffed them into his pocket and nodded, his deep purple lips curling up like strips of liver into an oily, commiserative smile. "Who the hell could figure the chalk horse getting beat?" he asked me. "Did you see those workouts, Frankie? Fantastic time, huh? Well, what the hell. Horses are like people. Unpredictable. That's what makes the sport, huh? Say, by the way, I seen on TV your pal Nockerman got blown away."

"How do you know I knew Nockerman?"

"Didn't I see you at the track with him a couple of times? He ran with some funny people, didn't he?"

Funny people in Freedo's lexicon meant non-Outfit thugs.

"I don't know who he ran with. We weren't that tight."

"Okay, Frank, I understand." His hands flew up in a gesture of conciliation. "I'm just saying I seen him around town with some funny people. Anyway, the hell with it. Why don't you stick around. Play some cards, shoot some dice. Unwind a little."

"All right," I said. "Maybe I'll play some cards."

Freedo smiled again, whacked me on the back again. "Good, Frankie, good. There's a game goin' on in the back."

I walked toward the back of the apartment. Slouched in a corner in a metal folding chair, browsing through a newspaper, was Bruno, the house muscle and collection engineer. I could smell him from where I stood, ten feet away: garlic and Selsun Blue. He looked like a sausage encased in blue serge. He glared at me as I walked by, his face reptilian with its scaly skin, blunt features, and greenish cast from lack of sunshine.

I bowed slightly from the waist in his direction, my hands before me in an attitude of prayer, the way they greet one another in India. "Namastay." He blinked, then turned back to his reading.

As I loosened my tie and took a seat at the blackjack table, I felt that familiar rolling in my bowels, the visceral turbulence which precedes the drama of gambling. The players greeted me with grunts and nods. One heavy winner was more effusive. "Don't sit to my right," he muttered. "You'll fuck up the sequence of my cards."

I told the man politely, "I don't mind moving at all."

Freedo sent over a drink. I lit up a long panatela and watched the dealer shuffle. Now, the pure joy of play, the quickening of the senses, the trance of concentration, the mental mechanics of counting cards, calculating odds against the draw, the summoning of all my art and science against blind chance and its capricious humor. Will God favor my endeavor tonight?

Not right away, apparently. I lost eight consecutive hands, and won the ninth with thirteen when the dealer busted. I felt a little better then; I was no longer a virgin. " 'Bout time you took one," said the man to my left.

For two hours the cards fell against me with seeming malice aforethought. The money flew from my hands into the black hole, the insatiable maw that eats losers. By midnight I was broke, down seven yards.

Freedo suddenly appeared at my side. "Need some cash, Frankie? How much?" I summoned my will and said no.

I drove home through a sporadic drizzle, sick with self-contempt, yet almost elated: loser's syndrome. I took another silent, solemn oath to quit. Back in my apartment I checked the phone answering machine. No calls. I poured myself a double Jack Daniel's, dropped in two ice cubes, walked into my bedroom and turned on the television. I kicked off my shoes and flopped on the bed. I sipped my whiskey and watched a late-night replay of *Life-styles of the Rich and Famous*.

In a minute or two I started dozing. Before I drifted away, I felt under the bed for my Smith & Wesson .45 automatic and the cannister of Mace I keep within easy reach. Just a little something to help me sleep.

I hate to hear the phone ring too early on a Sunday morning. It's either bad news or business, and who needs either, especially on the Sabbath when you're still in bed and half asleep.

"Hello," I mumbled, more by reflex than will.

"Frank Wolf?" It was a female voice, a deep contralto, well-cultivated to make an impression on others, but still not entirely free of the sound that said: raised in Chicago.

I woke up another degree. "Yes, this is Frank Wolf."

"I'm Abel Nockerman's ex-wife. I understand you once did some work for my former husband. He mentioned your name a few times and said he trusted you. I'd like to hire you to find out who murdered him."

"Why don't we talk about it Monday at my office."

"No. I'd rather you come to my apartment this evening. We'll have dinner together. Is seven all right? I want you to get started right away."

I needed the money desperately, and Nockerman was a man who always interested me, so I agreed. She gave me her address, a high-rise on Lake Shore Drive in that ultraswank block between Division and Elm. "Be prompt, Mr. Wolf," she added before hanging up.

I drove south through neon twilight, the sun not quite down, the streetlights not yet on; but the storefront signs and electronic billboards blazed and blinked into the gathering darkness.

I turned the radio to the old-time music station, songs of

the forties and fifties. Easy on the ear and brain. The performers seemed sane and sober, at least on the records. The music was sweet, the sentiments sweeter. The lyrics made sense and usually rhymed.

I swung the car onto the Outer Drive, merging into the endless chain of traffic rushing toward downtown Chicago. Irascible drivers screamed at me soundlessly through closed windows, gave me the finger in mute derogation of my driving. The motorized fight-or-flight syndrome.

As I cruised along the lakefront, watching the glass-clad towers on the right, the heaving waters of manganese blue and green on the left, I felt what I always feel driving this route: some inexplicable exhilaration, inspired perhaps by the harmonies between the man-made and the natural, which seemed especially beautiful along these few miles of urban shoreline. Further south the metallic brutalities of the East Chicago steelworks and its noxious outpourings ravage the air and water. When I hit that stretch, it's terminal depression and a sense of suffocation.

I parked in the garage below Mrs. Nockerman's building. The attendant looked at my old two-door Chevy with an air of contempt.

"How long you gonna be?" he asked.

"An hour, more or less."

"Want me to hose down your car?"

"Sure," I said.

"I get off at eight. Want to take care of me now?"

I gave him a fin and he smiled graciously.

"How about a wax job? Ten bucks extra."

"No, thanks," I told him. "I like the dull finish."

I stood before the garage security door and identified myself to the lobby doorman as a TV camera transmitted my picture. I was buzzed in, and as I walked across the spongy carpeting the doorman nodded at me from behind a tilted video console of a half-dozen flickering screens. In his gold-braided hat and quasi-military uniform he looked like an admiral on the bridge of the *Enterprise*.

"I've already phoned Mrs. Nockerman," he said. "You can go right up."

I rode the elevator to the twentieth floor, staring at another cyclopean video camera in a corner high on the wall. The silent sentinel watches everything. You can't even scratch your ass without the gatekeeper seeing it on his monitor.

I rang the bell at 20S, face-to-face with a head-level fish-eye peeper. I waited a moment, then heard the heavy bolts shoved open, the sturdy dead bolts turning, the clatter of thick chains unlatched.

The door finally opened.

"Mr. Wolf, how nice of you to come."

"Mrs. Nockerman?"

"Yes, come in."

In her prime she must have been beautiful. Now she looked like an aging Joan Crawford: slender; a cold, aristocratic calm in her speech and movements; black hair worn shoulder length; eyes unusually wide in deep, shadowed sockets; lips a bit too glossy. She must have been forty-five or so; her skin stretched unnaturally taut across her creaseless, bony face, sign of a recent lift that had yet to loosen up and settle. She wore dark-chocolate slacks and a tan silk blouse with billowing sleeves, open at the throat, her upper chest spattered with freckles. She led me through a short corridor and then we turned into an immense living room with broad panes of floor-to-ceiling glass that overlooked the lake. I sat near the windows at the end of a huge C-shaped couch plushly upholstered and covered in brown velour. She sat opposite me in a leather-and-chrome Barcelona chair.

"Will you have a drink?" she asked.

"Later," I said.

"Then let's get right to the point. I want you to find the man who killed my husband."

"The police are working on it," I said. "They'll find him."

"The police?" she huffed. "They'll poke around for a week or two, and if there's no pressure, they'll give up on it."

Despite its enormous size the room was rather Spartan, the impulse to overdecorate a space that large was admirably restrained. On the cold white walls hung several large abstract paintings, thick with impasto and reckless, sweeping brushstrokes. Arrayed on a low, horizontal bookcase was a small army of pre-Columbian figurines, red clay creatures with narrow-eyed, vaguely Oriental faces. The incidental furnishings—the tables, chairs, lamps—were all burnished metal or hand-rubbed wood, cut in clean, crisp Bauhaus lines. The place was not ostentatious yet it reeked of new money, calculated taste, social ambition.

"You live here alone?"

"Yes."

"It's so big," I said.

"I like to entertain. Abel and I lived together here. We had some marvelous parties."

"Did you love your husband?"

"I did for many years, yes. Then it all fell apart." She said it without emotion.

"Why?"

"I don't know. Mid-life crisis, business pressures. He lost a lot of money one year. He was terribly depressed. Then the following year he made more than he ever had before. Do you know the commodity business? It's crazy. There's tremendous stress. You make a wrong move, you can lose a fortune."

"I've heard that."

"Will you take the case, Mr. Wolf?"

"Yes." I wanted to find out who had killed this boyhood hero of mine, and why. And then, of course, there was the money.

"Good. What'll it cost me?"

I quoted her my daily fee. "Plus expenses," I added. "I'll need a month's pay in advance."

"A month? Isn't that excessive? What if it doesn't take you that long?"

"Then you've paid me a bonus for speed and efficiency."

"All right," she said. "I'll give you a check tonight."

"Fine. I'll give you a written progress report at the end of every week."

"That won't be necessary. You can just tell me what you find out. By the way, will you be sharing your information with the police?"

"Not necessarily."

"Good. My dear, departed husband was a rotten weasel. I'd hate for my daughter to find out what kind of man he was. By the way, she'll be dining with us tonight. Just remember, she adored her father, and I don't want her to be hurt."

"No, of course not. But if I break the case before the cops

do, I'll have to turn it over to them anyway. I may even need their help somewhere down the road."

"Try to avoid that. When the police have information it always gets into the newspapers. And it's never accurate, especially if it's negative. I don't want Tina reading a lot of salacious gossip about her father."

"I understand Tina found the body."

"Yes." She nodded, grim-faced, reflecting perhaps on the horror of her daughter's discovery.

"How'd she react?"

"She was devastated, of course."

"What about the insurance money?"

Her eyebrows went up like birds taking flight. She recrossed her legs.

"Well, you certainly get right to the point. Abel left me a small policy. Half a million, with the double indemnity. That's it, nothing else. Tina collects on the term. One million, I believe. And of course, she inherits everything."

"The brokerage business too?"

"Yes, Abel had no partners. Tina is now sole owner."

"I understand some money was taken from Mr. Nockerman's apartment."

She seemed surprised. "Why yes, I was getting to that. How did you know?"

"The police had me in yesterday. They asked me some questions about the work I did for your husband."

"Really? What's that got to do with anything? Anyway, Abel always kept a lot of money around the house. Sometimes several hundred thousand."

"Why so much?"

"From the business, I suppose. I want that money recovered. It belongs to Tina. The man who killed Abel probably took it."

"It's possible," I said politely. "Assuming there *was* money."

"And remember," Mrs. Nockerman said, "I'd like to avoid all this getting into the newspapers."

"Sooner or later the press will get it," I told her.

"Not the sordid details, I hope. Not all of it."

"All of what?"

There was an instant of hesitation before she answered.

"His women, his gambling, the way he threw money around."

"Mrs. Nockerman, how old is your daughter?"

"Twenty-four."

"Then she probably knows all about her father. If she loves him, she'll forgive him, if she hasn't already. Was he an honest businessman?"

"Scrupulously, as far as I know." There was no irony in her voice.

"How long have you been divorced?" I asked.

"Eight years."

I shot a quick, quizzical glance around the room, mutely admiring its understated opulence. "How do you support yourself?"

"I had a very good settlement. No thanks to Abel. He wanted the divorce, but he made it very difficult and unpleasant. Do you know how much money he made over the years? Millions. But I had to fight for every cent. Thank God I had a marvelous lawyer, a man as smart and ruthless as Abel. And I don't mind telling you, I've managed my money very carefully and made some excellent investments. I got custody of Tina, you know. She was just sixteen and she took it very hard. Abel set up a substantial trust fund for her. She comes into it later this year."

"Tell me about Mr. Nockerman's business."

"It's quite modest by LaSalle Street standards, but very successful. All his clients are very wealthy. Abel advised them on the markets and managed their trading accounts. He also did a lot of trading for himself, down on the floor."

"You mean in the pits?"

"Yes, in the pits, executing customer orders and speculating for himself. He was quite a shooter, as they say on LaSalle Street—obsessed, in fact. In the early days he lost huge amounts of money. But for years now he's been on a winning streak. His brokerage business pretty much took care of itself. There's an office manager, a man named Teddy Lane. He runs the day-to-day operation."

"I'll have to talk to him," I said. "Can you arrange it for me?"

"I'll telephone him tomorrow."

"Will you sell the business now?"

"That's up to Tina. The business is hers. But I've advised her to dispose of it."

"Have you seen your husband recently?"

"A few months ago."

"Did he mention any problems he might be having?"

"Not a word. We didn't get together very often after the divorce and when we did it was strictly business—legalities, insurance problems, Tina."

"Did you know any of his girlfriends?"

"Those bitches he ran with? No." Her voice was cold.

"You know his business associates?"

"No."

"What about friends? Any possibilities there?"

"Those envious bastards. They were all jealous of Abel's success."

"Jealous enough to kill him?"

"Yeah, kill him with upsmanship. You know that crowd. All very competitive. Someone buys a forty-foot yacht, the next buys a fifty-footer. Abel would buy a sixty-footer and tell 'em, 'eat your hearts out.' "

"Who were his enemies?"

"None that I know of."

"He ever screw someone in a deal? Stiff a creditor?"

"Abel was a lousy husband, but an honest man."

I knew men like that. They'd cheat on their wives eight days a week, and never dream of cheating at cards—unless they were sure they'd get away with it.

"He ever steal someone's girlfriend?" I asked.

"Probably. He was disgusting. Like a goat in heat."

The doorbell rang like the chimes of Big Ben. Mrs. Nockerman called out to some unseen servant in another room, "Hilda, will you get that, please." Then she told me, "It's Tina. This has all been very difficult for her. Let's not get into a lot of unpleasantness at the dinner table."

"I'll have to ask her some questions."

"I know, but take it easy."

A moment later Tina made her entrance. She flowed into the room all energy and relaxed self-assurance, arms swinging loosely, thick brunette hair jouncing lightly just above her shoulders with each long stride as she came toward us. Some quality in the atmosphere suddenly changed with her presence. As she bent to kiss her mother I caught a whiff of her perfume, an astringent fragrance somewhere between gardenias and a martini. Then she turned to me, smiling, anticipating.

"Tina, this is Mr. Wolf," Mrs. Nockerman said.

I stood. She offered her hand. It seemed to hum against my palm with some subtle vibration. She was tall and we were almost eye to eye. I could feel the warmth of her body emanating from beneath her lavender silk blouse. Tina was a gem, radiant with health and vitality, slender yet full-breasted, an extraordinary creature at once girlish and womanly. She looked somewhat like her mother, but was much more attractive, and not just because she was younger. Her skin was smooth, with no excessive applications of makeup, her eyes black as anthracite, her lips plump and finely wrought, just barely touched with a tint of color, her long neck tilted slightly as she looked at me.

"Do you remember me?" she asked.

"No," I said. "I'm afraid I don't."

"I met you once. Years ago, in Daddy's office. I was in my early teens, and you made quite an impression on me. Especially after Daddy told me what you did for a living."

"Yes, I think I remember. I'm sorry about your father."

"Thank you," she said, her mouth lifting into that sad, faraway smile with which the bereaved accept expressions of sympathy.

"Shall we eat?" said Mrs. Nockerman.

We sat in the dining room at a glass table with tubular legs of chrome, Mrs. Nockerman at the head, Tina on her right. I sat opposite Tina, and through the large windows I could see the gentle curve of Lake Shore Drive as it veered east past the Drake and the ornate facades of the splendid old buildings that faced on Oak Street Beach. Hilda, a robust Teutonic matron of Wagnerian dimensions, served dinner.

The fare was luscious. We began with a small shrimp salad, properly chilled and noisily crisp, accompanied by an exquisitely dry Graves. The chateaubriand was sliced in thin slabs and flanked by garden-fresh green beans and glazed carrots julienne. The second bottle of wine was a superlative, full-bodied Cabernet Sauvignon. It was all very fancy and impressive. But I assumed Mrs. Nockerman and Tina didn't eat like this every night, not with their health-spa figures to maintain.

As if reading my mind, Mrs. Nockerman remarked, "Once a week we indulge ourselves this way. Tina and I just love good food."

They both ate like Europeans, knife in the right hand, fork in the left. And apparently grief had not dulled their appetites.

We chatted about trivialities for a few minutes and then Mrs. Nockerman turned to Tina. "I've hired Mr. Wolf to investigate your father's murder." She swallowed a mouthful and took a sip of wine. "He's going to have to ask you a lot of questions, dear, and I'm afraid it might be somewhat painful for you. But I want this thing resolved as soon as possible. You'll give Mr. Wolf all the help you can, won't you, dear." Her tone seemed more like a command than a request.

"Yes, of course," Tina said, looking up at me from her plate.

"I don't want to spoil your dinner," I told her. "Maybe we can meet somewhere next week and talk about it."

"Fine," she said. "I own an art gallery on Michigan Avenue in the six-eighteen building. It's called Quest. Maybe you can come in tomorrow."

"Can we make it Tuesday? For lunch? I'm going to your father's brokerage firm tomorrow. You won't forget to arrange that for me, will you, Mrs. Nockerman?"

"Tina should really make the call. It's her company now."

"I'll phone Teddy, Mr. Wolf," Tina said. "And I'll meet you Tuesday at twelve at the gallery."

Addressing both of them, I said, "I know the police have been all over Mr. Nockerman's apartment, but I'd like to look at it myself. I understand you have the key, Tina."

"You want to see Daddy's place?" Her voice was a blend of surprise and outrage. No doubt she thought of me as an intruder, an insensitive stranger asking for permission to desecrate her late father's living quarters by nosing around in its secret crannies.

"You're certainly welcome to look around, Mr. Wolf," she said stiffly.

"Next week sometime okay?"

"Whenever it's convenient for you."

Hilda cleared away our plates and brought dessert, an orange marmalade soufflé laced with Grand Marnier, garnished with whipped cream light as goose down.

"Tell me about your father, Tina."

"He was a wonderful man," she said. "I wish I had been a better daughter. Mom always said he was too preoccupied with business. Maybe that's true, but he always had time for me. I'm an only child, you know, and maybe I'm a bit spoiled. Daddy gave me everything, whatever I wanted—cars, clothing, an excellent education, the money to start my art gallery. He sent all his friends over to buy from me."

"Your father's friends? Can you give me a list? Names, addresses, phone numbers?"

"Yes," she said. "And you'll be able to meet most of them at my gallery. I'm opening a new show in a few weeks and they'll all be there."

I finished my dessert and sipped steaming black coffee. I felt pleasantly full from the superb meal.

"Would you like something else?" Mrs. Nockerman asked me. Smiling, with her head tilted upward, she looked very much like her daughter. "You look at me so funny, Mr. Wolf. Remember, I'm not a grieving widow. I'm not terribly upset about his death." She turned to Tina. "Forgive me, dear, you know I've always been perfectly frank."

"Yes, Mother, that's one of your sterling qualities."

Mrs. Nockerman turned back to me. "I know you get paid by the week, Mr. Wolf, but I'll pay you a substantial bonus if you clear this thing up in a hurry."

"Let me tell you about the detective business," I said. "I don't have subpoena power. I can't compel people to talk to me. And I don't twist arms. That slows things down a little."

"I imagine. Well, if you need to bribe someone for information, you can come to me for the money."

"Don't ever tell that to another P.I., Mrs. Nockerman. That might wind up costing you a few bucks. With no guarantee you'll get what you paid for."

"Yes, I understand," she nodded. "Will you excuse me now? I'll be back in a moment."

I watched Mrs. Nockerman stride from the room—long, purposeful steps, devouring space and time.

In a moment she returned and handed me a check

across the table. "One month's wages," she said. I didn't like the way she said *wages;* it made me feel like a servant. I looked at the check and noticed that her signature was a combination of upper and lower case letters. "Be sure to keep track of your expenses," she said.

"Thank you." I folded the check and put it in my pocket. They both escorted me to the door.

"I'll see you Tuesday, Tina," I said.

"Yes," she said, smiling. "I'm looking forward to it."

So was I.

Mrs. Nockerman said, "You'll probably hear some strange things about Abel once you start looking into this. But I'll tell you something, beneath his superficial flash, Abel was really quite average."

5

The Nockerman I knew was anything but average. Always impeccably tailored, even in sports clothes, always it seemed just recently returned from a weekend in the tropics, or perhaps just fresh from the tanning salon. He was thinner and more physically fit than most men his age, with more assurance in his voice, more swagger in his walk, more competitive, more arrogant. The archetypical commodity trader—he had a sense of himself as lucky, gifted, smarter than others, more in tune with his senses and physicality, and in possession of more balls than other people, especially his colleagues in the pits.

He was chronically hoarse, an occupational hazard of the pits and its requirement for open outcry. The condition is like singer's nodes, lots of traders are afflicted. With his rough, deep voice, his flat Chicago accent, his deliberately crude language, he sounded more like a thug than what he really was: a Phi Beta Kappa with a master's degree in accounting.

He was wild, erratic, his moods fluctuating like the markets. At times he was insanely generous; some gamblers have that in common with commodity traders, along with their need to impress people.

I saw him give a hundred-dollar bill to a panhandler on LaSalle Street. Nockerman laughed demonically as the bum studied the note in total bewilderment, then shuffled quickly away without lifting his eyes to look upon his benefactor or uttering a "thank you," afraid perhaps that the giver would discover his mistake and demand his money back.

But Nockerman also had a darker side.

I had run into him late one afternoon after the markets had closed, and he dragged me to a favorite haunt of his, a traders' hangout called The Margin Call. It was a dark, cavernous bar and restaurant. High on the wall at either side of the room was a broad translux display where commodity prices ran continuously during market hours so that traders could have a bite and a drink without missing a market tick. When trading ended for the day, closing prices for every commodity at every major exchange—the Board of Trade, the Merc, the Mid-America, the Comex, and others—were endlessly displayed in a running ribbon of light.

There were nods and greetings as Nockerman and I sat down with a group at a big round table in the back. They were commodity traders, acquaintances of Nockerman, but I read in their faces that they were not pleased by his arrival. He ordered a round of drinks for everyone, and I sipped my Jack Daniel's as I listened to their chatter. They seemed to me like high school kids, high on their own bravado, competing to outdrink and outbrag each other. As they talked, they posed before their peers, flashing the emblems of their material success: the Rolex watches; the immense diamond solitaires in platinum settings; the long, two-dollar Dunhills clenched between capped teeth, smoked not even a fourth of the way down before being replaced by a new one.

One guy was saying, "I got comped everything, the suite, the jet, even the limo to O'Hare. What I drop? Eighty-two kay, I think. For me, that's a run of luck. I was up thirty hours straight, in the V.I.P. penthouse, playing baccarat with those Ay-rabs and Greeks, and Texas shit-kickers. But you know something? Same scene in Monte Carlo. 'Cept you get the European four-flushers, those assholes pretending they're royalty."

When the first guy stopped talking, another started.

"The G. took it all away. The movie shelter, the coal shelter, now they're fuckin' with the cattle shelter. I got two thousand acres in Montana with livestock. What the fuck am I gonna do if they kill the cattle break?"

"Whaddaya worried about?" someone said. "Long as the President's got cattle, nobody'll fuck with it."

Another guy: "Remember when gold hit eight-fifty an ounce? I dumped it right at the fuckin' top. That's the truth,

I swear. Seventeen bucks off the high, I take an oath, that's where I sold it. Over a thousand ounces. Un-fucking-believable, huh?"

Someone else: "I chartered a yacht used to belong to Onassis's cousin. . . ."

Nockerman whispered to me, "Versberg's his name. Real asshole."

Even sitting, Versberg seemed tall. He was lean, well tanned, about forty, with curly graying hair, eyes green and murky like unpolished jade, eyelids swollen by allergy or lack of sleep, giving him an Oriental look. He was saying: "Whole fucking crew came with it. Even a cook. Captain was a gloomy son-of-a-bitch. Hotter 'n hell and he always had his goddamn jacket on. Like he's Admiral Hornblower or someone. We used to all lay naked on the afterdeck, the sun beatin' on us, do a couple lines, get a little lucky. Right out in the open. Fucking crew sees it all, not a blink, not a peep. You ever get laid on the Mediterranean? At sunset? Man, it was so beautiful, it was unreal."

Suddenly, without apparent provocation, Nockerman sprang to his feet, threw his drink in Versberg's face. "You're a fuckin' cheat," he barked.

Versberg blanched. His hands flew up to his face in reflex. He pushed himself away from the table, his chair tumbling backward as he tried to stand. "Hey, Nocky, I thought we settled . . ."

Nockerman lunged at him, chopping with open hands. "Nocky's stoned," someone shouted. Versberg dropped to the floor, curled up knees and chest, clutching his sides and groaning in agony. Nockerman leaped on him. I grabbed Nocky from behind, wrestling him into a hammerlock. "Abel, stop, you'll kill him."

With my arm tight against Nockerman's throat, I pulled him off Versberg. He was trembling, and screaming incoherently as I backed him away. Then I relaxed my grip and he let me shove him gently through the silent crowds as we moved through the room and out the door.

Later that evening, over steaks at Barneys, Nockerman, calm and smiling, said, "If you hadn't stopped me, Frank, I woulda killed that bastard. He fucked me over in the pits. Caused me some real bad out-trades."

"What's an out-trade?"

"You make a trading mistake on the floor, you settle it
outside. Trouble is, it costs you money. Look, it happens.
People fuck up. No big deal. But this Versberg asshole kept
sockin' it to me. Three, four times, on purpose. Little game
he plays. I warned him. But you know, some people don't
learn easy. You got to stick the lesson up their ass."

Recalling the incident, I made a note to interview Versberg first chance I had.

Okay, I had a new case. I bought fresh batteries for the
tape recorder, film for the Nikon and Polaroid, and ammuni-
tion for my handguns. Also, I took the usual oaths and uttered the customary vows. A good P.I. should be like an athlete: clean mind, clean body, a paragon of mental, physical,
and spiritual fitness. That's my ideal. The reality is somewhat different.

So I started to work, keeping in mind the old Heisenberg
Uncertainty Principle of particle physics: the act of observing something changes it. The same holds true in any investigation.

Monday morning was cool and cloudless, the sky a deep cerulean blue. I left my car in a city parking lot and walked briskly south down LaSalle Street, nudged and jostled by the streaming crowds. A sharp, astringent wind blew in from the lake, heaving and snapping in powerful gusts. I crossed against the light at Madison, dodging cars, buses, honking taxis. On either side I was flanked by huge banks, gloomy, ponderous structures with Palladian facades of dirty white marble or earth-brown masonry. The anal-retentive architecture of old financial districts everywhere. At the foot of the street stood the Board of Trade building, a gray tower of some forty stories atop which presides a colossal statue of an ancient deity: Ceres, Roman goddess of agriculture, a green weathered icon in the Art Deco style.

As I passed the broad glass panes of a posh menswear shop I caught a reflected glimpse of myself. At thirty-eight, no middle-age paunch, no postural slouch, hair still dark brown and without a trace of gray, although not quite as thick as it used to be. A short vertical scar bisects my left eyebrow. My nose has been broken three times—twice as a reporter, once as a P.I.—so it's just a millimeter flat at the bridge and not quite symmetrical. I made a mental note to resume my regular workouts. The nature of my business— and my healthy vanity—requires that I keep my weight down.

I pushed through the revolving doors at the Board of Trade building and walked across the enormous lobby toward the elevators, stepping upon the inlaid floor designs, which symbolize in modern abstractions the type of commerce conducted here: sheaves of wheat, bundles of oats, stalks of golden corn.

The elevator was stuffed with traders in their poplin jackets, ID badges pinned to their lapels, the uniform required by the exchange for admission to the trading floor. They gibbered to one another in the strange lingo of the futures market. "Beans opened down limit and locked. And me long with twenty contracts. Not a chance in hell of getting out."

I got off the elevator, turned left, and walked to the end of the corridor. The sign on the door said:

NOCKERMAN COMMODITIES, INC.
MEMBER: CHICAGO BOARD OF TRADE
CHICAGO MERCANTILE EXCHANGE

"My name is Frank Wolf," I told the receptionist. "I have an appointment with Mr. Lane."

"Yes, he's expecting you." She buzzed Lane on the intercom and a moment later he came walking into the reception room, a short, stocky, almost totally bald man of forty-five or so, in blue pinstriped vest and shirtsleeves. A slight, graceful swagger in his gait suggested that perhaps he had been a college athlete—a track man, maybe, or a swimmer.

He shook my hand, squeezed a little too hard, a common trait among the not-too-tall. "I hope this won't take too much time, Mr. Wolf."

"Just a few questions."

"All right, let's get on with it."

He led me into a rather large room past rows of empty desks in perfect alignment. At the front of the room was a huge electronic quote board, twitching and clicking with the latest market prices. Along one wall was a mammoth bulletin board dripping with sheets and broad ribbons of paper: photocopied articles from the *Wall Street Journal, Barrons,* the *Journal of Commerce,* U.S.D.A. crop reports and production estimates. Along the back wall stood a commodity news service teletype machine humming like a manic bee, spewing forth a broad ribbon of paper, which trailed on the floor. On the wall above the machine hung two giant maps, of America and the world, full-color Mercator projections superimposed with little black symbols—cows, pigs, ears of corn, bags of coffee. Domestic and international commodities at a glance.

Lane's office was a cubicle of glass and steel partitions without a ceiling. He sat at his desk and I sat opposite him.

"Christ," he sighed. "It's been pandemonium here. I've been on the phone with clients continuously since Nockerman got killed."

"What's that big room back there?" I asked.

"We used to have a large sales crew a few years ago. It got to be too much hassle, so Nockerman let them all go."

He slurped from a styrofoam cup whose rim he had chewed and bitten to shreds. "Would you like some coffee?"

"No, thanks," I said.

To Lane's right on his desk stood a video display terminal. Commodity prices flashed upon it in a green flickering light. As we talked, his eyes repeatedly flew away from me to the screen. Then he'd glance back at me for a few seconds, only to return compulsively once again to the ever-changing numbers on the tube.

"Gotta keep an eye on the market," he said. "I'm servicing Nockerman's accounts. Honest to God, I'm sick over this."

"Did Nockerman know all his clients?" I asked.

Lane, impatient, answered, "No, no. Just the big ones. The people he brought in himself, or the referrals. We got a lot of Mickey Mouse business, accounts we brought in by mail and telephone solicitation, the way all brokerage firms do."

"What's 'Mickey Mouse'?"

"Fifty, seventy-five thousand. Right away they get burned out. Six months, a year, they got a zero balance. Losses and commissions. But understand something, we never churn and burn. Nockerman didn't allow it."

"Churn and burn?"

"Yeah," Lane said. "Trading excessively just for the commissions. Most of the accounts were discretionary. That means Nockerman managed them as he pleased. Bought and sold whatever he wanted, any amount, without the client's prior consent. Common arrangement in the business."

"Got any ideas about who killed Nockerman?"

"None," he said.

"Got any hunches?" I was a believer in hunches. They've

made some of my biggest wins, helped me crack some of the most impenetrable cases. Hunches were the evidence that we possessed a sixth sense. The problem was distinguishing between the authentic hunch and the random notion without merit that masquerades as the real thing.

"Hunches? No."

"What about current or ex-employees?" I asked. "Was someone fired recently?"

"No."

"How about Nockerman's girlfriend? She a possible?"

"Rita? I've met her," Lane said. "But I don't know her. Beautiful woman. Classy."

"Were they getting along with one another?"

"I don't know. Nockerman didn't confide in me."

"You know any clients lost a lot of money lately?"

Lane shrugged. "What's a lot of money? A hundred grand? Two hundred? It's all relative. Sure, some of our clients dropped big numbers. No surprise in this business. But Christ, they're loaded. Most of 'em take their hits without a blink. Yeah, they piss and moan, but they always come back. Playing the market's a compulsion with some people."

"I'd like you to compile a list for me," I said. "Clients of Nockerman who lost a hundred grand or more in the last couple years. Names and addresses too."

"What? You think some guy is going to murder his broker 'cause he blew a hundred grand in the market? That's crazy."

"Will you get me the list?"

"Sure, I'll get a computer printout. Come back tomorrow about nine. I'll have it for you."

"How'd you get along with Nockerman?"

"Me? Just fine. I ran the whole business for him for twenty-one years."

"You shoulda been a partner by now," I said.

"Yeah, I guess."

"Piss you off a little?"

"Not much," he said.

"You keep the books too?"

"Yeah, so what?"

"Speculate a little for yourself once in a while?"

"Sure," Lane said. "We all do."

"Ever borrow a couple bucks from Nockerman to cover a margin call or offset a loss?"

"Never."

"Ever help yourself to a little Nockerman money and doctor the books until you could pay it back?"

"Come on, Wolf, you're jerking off."

"You ready for an independent audit?"

"An audit? What the hell for?"

"Whenever a man with business partners is murdered I always order an audit."

"Yeah, well go ahead," he said. His voice seemed assured, without stress. "Just give me advance notice so I can contact our accountants."

"Maybe next week," I said. I got up from my chair and told him, "I'll be back tomorrow morning for that list. Thanks for your help."

Calmly and very slowly, Lane stood up, his face pale and solemn, like a prisoner in the dock about to give testimony.

"Wolf, I swear on my children, the books are straight, even the petty cash. You can't steal from a place like this. Everything's too tight. Nockerman went over the books like a hawk. He's a wizard with numbers. I made a good living here, I like the business. Word gets out my books might be funny, I'm dead, I'll never get another job. You bring in auditors and the whole street'll know."

"All right," I said. "We'll say it's a liquidation audit. Miss Nockerman wants to sell the business and needs to determine its value on the market. How's that, okay?"

He sat down. "Thanks, Wolf. You're such a generous guy. But who the fuck'll believe it?"

☐ I left Lane, rode the express elevator down, and bought all the papers at the lobby newsstand, including the *Wall Street Journal* and the *Daily Racing Form*. I remembered then that Versberg had an office nearby on LaSalle Street, so I phoned him and asked if I could come over. He said he couldn't see me, especially on such short notice, but I told him we'd have to talk sooner or later, so it might as well be now.

"All right," he said. "But I can't make a whole goddamn day out of it."

Versberg met me at his office door and led me past the desks and filing cabinets into a huge suite at the rear of the corridor that had been outfitted like a private residence, with lots of ersatz Art Deco furniture in washed-out mauves and grays.

"You like?" he asked. "This is the living room. I got a complete two-bedroom apartment here. Right next to my office. I don't live here, you understand. S'just a convenience. Hot tub, Jacuzzi, the whole *schmear*. Grab a snooze, grab a little *shtup*, whatever I want. Nice, huh? Whad'll ya drink?"

"Nothing right now."

Versberg poured himself a big Stolichnaya on ice and we sat in massive chrome-and-velour easy chairs, facing each other across a glass-topped coffee table.

"Yeah, poor Nockerman. Rest his soul," Versberg said. "Like excuse me for not breaking down."

"I was at the Margin Call that night," I said.

"What night?" Versberg asked. "The night Nocky

jumped me? Yeah, I think I remember. You the guy pulled him off me?"

I nodded.

"You don't think *I* blew him away?

"Tell me about Nockerman."

"Made boo coo money. Just like me. " 'Course, I'm sane. Nocky was loco."

"What happened between you?"

"I made a mistake in the pits. Big soybean trade. I sold, he bought. I wrote it down wrong on my card. Nocky thought I did it on purpose. To fuck him. You kiddin' me? I need that kind of grief? You know what I own? Nursing homes, for Christ sakes, ranchland in Montana, a fucking condo in Maui. I need Nocky's money? Let me tell you about Nocky, he's a one-upsman, always trying to better you. Like that story he put out about the millions he made when the market crashed. That's why he got pissed about this. It wasn't the money, believe me. Although there was plenty involved. Anyway, we settled up, and I apologized. I thought it was over. Few months later he chop-socky's me in the Margin Call."

"He had trouble with other traders too?"

"Probably. Nocky was a mega-putz. But I'll tell you, people in this business get pissed off at a guy, they don't murder him, they blacklist him. Could be just as bad. A man can't make a trade anymore. Nobody takes his action in the pits. You follow? They won't even look at him. He can't buy nothing, he can't sell nothing."

"That happen to Nockerman?"

"In a limited way. I shut him out. Maybe a few others did too. But the man still traded. I mean, I stood next to him in the bean pit and saw him do business."

"Did he use drugs?"

"Who knows. Lots of people do in this business. It's no big secret. You read in the paper about the big bust recently? What'd they grab, six, eight people? Traders, runners, whatever. Tip of the iceberg, believe me. I seen people on the floor, fuckin' blind. You wonder how in hell they handle a deck. But what the hell, the pressure in this business can kill ya. So people feed their nose. Whaddya gonna do?" He shrugged.

"You ever hear of any other trouble Nockerman had?"

"Sure, Nocky hassled lots of people. But getting angry's

one thing, killing a man's another. 'Course, there's lots of heavy money around. Why couldn't a guy with a grudge against Nocky hire a professional and have him hit? Man with enough balls and money might do something like that. Interesting idea, huh?"

"You know people capable of that?"

"Capable? Definitely?"

"Who?"

"Who?" he repeated. "What? I'm going to accuse someone? Like I said, the people Nocky fucked with just walked away. Turned their backs on the man. That's all I know. 'Course, after the big stock-market crash a lot of traders and speculators couldn't make their margin calls, so they went to the street for money. I'm talking juice. Far as I know, Nocky came through the dive without a scratch. Commodities was his game, not stocks. But who the hell knows? Maybe he borrowed Outfit cash, couldn't keep up the payments, so they pulled the plug on him."

"Nocky on juice? No, I don't think so," I said. I gave Versberg my business card. "Call me if you hear anything."

He tore it up into little pieces and dropped it into an ashtray. "Man that killed Nockerman should get the Nobel Prize."

It was a fine spring day, sunny, cool, and breezy, so when I finished with Versberg I decided to take a leisurely walk through the Loop. I needed some books on the commodity business, so I strolled down to Wabash Avenue to the big Kroch's and Brentano's south of Madison Street. Above me an El train screeched and rattled, its wheels gnashing steel against steel, grinding a fine metallic dust that fell from the elevated superstructure through lattices of shadow and sunlight. In Kroch's I found two books on the futures market, introductory volumes for beginners. I thought I should know a little something about Nockerman's business and how it worked.

8

I went back to my office and browsed through the *Tribune*. A story from New Mexico caught my eye:

MISSING CHICAGO MAN FOUND SLAIN
IN ALBUQUERQUE MOTEL ROOM

W. Mayne Angler, an assistant director of computer operations at a Chicago commodity clearinghouse, was found murdered early yesterday in a motel room in Albuquerque, New Mexico. According to Albuquerque police, he had been shot once in the head with a high-caliber pistol. Investigating detectives described the crime as a "gangland-style execution."

Records indicate Mr. Angler, a Chicago resident, had checked into the Albuquerque motel last Monday night under an assumed name. Documents and identification cards on his person, however, disclosed his real identity. Mr. Angler is survived by his wife, a daughter, and two grandchildren. Funeral arrangements are pending.

I read the story a second time. Was there a Nockerman connection here? Both men were murdered in similar fashion, both were in different ends of the same business, both were Chicagoans, and both were killed within days of each other. And Angler disappeared the day the Nockerman murder story broke in the papers and on TV news.

I telephoned Duffy at his office and told him Mrs. Nockerman hired me.

Silence for a beat or two before the reply. "She hired *you*? What the fuck for?"

"She thinks the guy who killed her ex-husband took some money from the apartment. She wants it back. Matter of fact, she wants me to wrap up the whole package."

Duffy did not sound happy. "Gettin' to be a habit with you, huh? Working for the Nockermans? Chicago P.D.'s not good enough for her? She was rude to my people during the interview."

"Listen to this." I read him the newspaper story about Angler.

"So what?"

"Could be a Nockerman tie-in here. Couple strong similarities. Both men in commodities. Both killed the same way. And Angler disappears on the day the Nockerman murder breaks in the press and TV news. Why don't you call the Albuquerque P.D. and see if they got a shell casing we can compare with the Nockerman brass? And while you're at it, see what else they got."

"That's a real long shot, Frank."

"You got something better right now?"

"No, but now that we're both on the Nockerman case, I will. You'll keep me informed and up-to-date on everything, right?"

"Bet on it."

When I finished talking with Duffy, I opened one of my new books on the commodities business and looked up *clearinghouse*:

> Every trade transacted on the floor of the exchange must go through the clearinghouse for settlement— money is collected from buyers and paid out to sellers, leaving a net balance of zero. Clearinghouse members pay a fee and a commission per trade.

If Nockerman's daily brokerage transactions were sent through Angler's clearinghouse, then maybe the two dead men knew each other.

I spent the next couple hours reading about the commodities futures business. It was basically a crap shoot, but an interesting gamble. You put up only a small percentage of the stake in margin money, which gives you tremendous leverage. So the payoffs could be immense. The losses too.

* * *

I grabbed an early dinner, then drove out to the Near West Side to play poker with some pals of mine. I caught good cards all night and squeezed them hard. By the end of the game I was up six yards and change. No great victory, but a small step back toward symmetry.

9

They were waiting for me in the foyer when I came home that night. There were two guys, one over six feet tall with a huge neck and shoulders, biceps like cantaloupes. He wore Levi's and a navy-blue polo shirt. Ten years ago he might have been a pro football player; he had the brick-wall look of a defensive lineman. The other guy was shorter, chunkier, in that physical limbo between muscle and fat which lasts a season or two before the flab starts to dominate. He may once have been a wrestler or boxer—there was scar tissue around his eyes and his ears were little cauliflowers. He wore a suit of gray seersucker, rumpled like pajamas.

"Wolf?" he asked as I walked in.

"No," I said. "Who're you?"

The little guy pulled a gun from his jacket, a short-barreled mag, and leveled it at my head. The big guy stepped behind me, clamped me in a hammerlock, while his partner gave me a one-handed rubdown.

"He ain't holdin'," the short guy said.

"Let's take a walk," the lineman said.

They marched me outside and around back into a narrow gangway between my apartment building and the one next to it.

The big guy still held me from behind and the little guy faced me.

"I ain't gonna need this," he said, and put away his gun. Then suddenly he stomped on my right foot. I thought I heard the cracking of tiny bones in my toes. I tried to kick him with my left foot, but he stepped inside it like a boxer dodging a jab and hit me six, seven times in the solar plexus —rapid, powerful blows with his left and right as if he were working a bag.

"Get off the Nockerman case," he said. He was panting.

I studied his face, trying to memorize it so that if I ever saw him again I could make a positive I.D.

"Did you hear me, motherfucker?" he said. "Get off the Nockerman case."

"I'm off," I said, gasping for air. "As of right now."

"Make sure, asshole. We're going to be watching you."

He hit me three more times in the stomach, but I saw it coming so I tensed my abdominals and his punches didn't hurt as bad as the first time. But I groaned and slumped against the big guy to show them I was hurt; no need to take more of a beating than necessary.

The big guy released me and I fell to the concrete pavement between buildings. They stepped over me and walked briskly out of the passageway, their bodies silhouetted against the diffuse glow of the street light, their heels clacking loudly on the cement.

I limped upstairs to my apartment and drank a big glass of orange juice. My foot was throbbing. I could wriggle the toes, but the pain was excruciating. Probably multiple fractures. My torso didn't feel so great either. But the pain didn't have that knife-in-the-lungs feeling that means broken ribs.

Later, I soaked in a hot bath, with my injured foot hanging over the tub, wrapped in a face towel and stuffed into a plastic bag filled with ice cubes. I sipped from a large tumbler of Jack Daniel's and tried to figure what it was all about —naturally, I had no intention of dropping the Nockerman case.

Question one: Who sent the message? I made a list of all the possibles: Lane, Versberg, Nocky's current and former girlfriends, all his old business associates, everyone he fucked over recently and back to year one, plus God knows who else.

Question two: What's my next move? The right play was to say nothing about the bashing to anyone and watch how people react to me. I trust my own perceptions, so if I saw something subtle but promising, I'd chase it.

I was not knocked out by the muscle unleashed on me. The beating was not severe and therefore not persuasive. They were either amateurs or third-rate semiprofessionals. And so was whoever hired them, I assumed. Which did not make these bush-league ballbusters any less dangerous.

10

At nine sharp the following morning I stopped to see Lane at Nockerman's brokerage office. There was no sign that he was surprised to see me, or that he noticed my slight limp.

He handed me a large manila envelope.

"Here are the names you wanted," he said. "In alphabetical order. There's a computer breakdown of all their trades since they became clients here, with a running profit and loss statement. All of 'em heavy losers."

"Ever hear of a guy named W. Mayne Angler? Worked at one of the big local clearinghouses."

His forehead furrowed. "Angler, Angler?" He shook his head. "Doesn't ring a bell."

I mentioned the name of Angler's clearinghouse. "You clear your trades through them?"

"Yeah," Lane said. "We do. What about it?"

"I don't know yet."

"Look, Wolf, the markets are gonna open. I gotta get to work."

"You send those two cretins after me?" I asked.

"What the hell are you talking about?"

I said nothing and just looked at him.

He looked back, silent, steady, not a crease or twitch in his face.

Finally, he said, "What is it, Wolf? What are you talking about?"

"Nothing," I said. "I'll be in touch."

I left my car in a parking lot and walked the few blocks to 618 Michigan Avenue. I consulted the lobby directory on the wall and found the listing for Tina's gallery.

The elevator reeked of Muzak. When the doors rolled open on the third floor, the Quest logo was directly opposite in thick, jigsawed wood affixed to the wall near the entrance. I walked into the gallery and strode briskly down the long, spacious corridor, my footfalls almost silent against the deep-pile carpeting.

At five minutes to noon the gallery was empty except for a young man sitting at a slender teakwood parsons table, murmuring into a telephone. As I approached, he laid a hand across the mouthpiece, lifted his head and asked, "Mr. Wolf?"

I nodded.

"I'm Tina's assistant. She's waiting for you. Go right in." He motioned with his head toward a closed door at the rear of the gallery.

On the walls hung the current exhibition, huge paintings of monochrome squares and rectangles floating on contrasting monochrome fields. The work was aseptic, hardedged, dull and monotonous as its color, without a trace of brushwork to suggest a human hand had created it.

I knocked on Tina's office door.

"Come in," she said.

She was hanging up the telephone as I entered. She rose and came around from her semicircular desk, smiling as she walked toward me, hand extended in greeting. She was beautiful in her navy-blue blazer and gray-flannel slacks. A silk paisley scarf was tied insouciantly at her neck, a matching kerchief was stuffed casually into her breast pocket. Her appearance was at once formal and breezy.

"You're limping, Mr. Wolf. What happened?"

"In-grown toenail," I replied. "You hungry?"

"Ravenous."

"Chinese?" I proposed.

"Fine."

Her assistant was still talking on the phone as we passed him on the way out. "Gerry," she told him, "I don't know how long I'll be. I'll call you." She then turned to me to ask, "What do you think of the show?"

"Interesting technique," I said, looking at a canvas. "It's done with a roller and house paint, isn't it?"

"No. Does it look that way?" She glanced at the painting, frowning.

"Just kidding."

We walked side by side up Michigan Avenue, bending forward into a gusting southeasterly wind. The streets were aswarm with the lunchtime crowd. The House of Hunan near Tribune Tower was packed, but the head waiter managed to find us a small table along the wall. We ordered Bombay martinis on the rocks and Kung Bao shrimp for two. The room resounded with conversation and the random clatter of cutlery.

Our drinks were brought and we sipped the icy liquid, looking at each other in silence across the table. There was something about her that was not quite as self-assured as she pretended, an uncertainty in her eyes, a hesitancy in her voice, as if on occasion she were feeling her way through life in the dark. Yet she was truly lovely, magnetically erotic. If I were somewhat younger, and she a little older and not my client's daughter, I could be interested. I mentally calculated the difference in our ages—I was not quite old enough to be her father.

"What are the chances of finding out who killed my father?" she asked.

"Right now they're good. That may change with time."

"If you felt you were wasting my mother's money, would you tell her?"

"You mean if I wasn't making progress in the investigation?"

She nodded.

"Yes," I said. "I would tell her."

Our food was brought and we commenced eating. "Tell me, Mr. Wolf, why would a man like you become a private investigator? You don't seem the type."

"What's the type?"

"You know, someone sneaky who does nasty things— follow people around, poke into their private lives."

"I used to be a reporter," I said. "Maybe that's why I got into this business, because it's so much like newspapering. You get onto a good story and follow it all the way through to the truth of things. I like that, it's satisfying. Although it's not always pleasant. But being a P.I. gave me freedom, independence, leisure, and ultimately—bankruptcy."

She laughed.

"I always wanted to write for a newspaper," I said. "After I got out of the army, I went to work for the *Chicago Daily Scrutinizer*. Police reporter. I liked the job, but I wanted to do some major investigative pieces, get my own column eventually. Anyway, I worked the police beat for a few years, moved up to general assignment, and just when I got comfortable with a weekly paycheck, the *Scrutinizer* folded. A great newspaper for over a hundred years, then gradually people stop reading it. That last day in the city room was like a wake. A newspaper folds, it's like somebody dies, somebody big and healthy you thought would be around forever. Couple of the older guys who spent their whole life with the paper were crying. I was pretty shook up myself. You work at a place long enough, you start feeling affection for it. My father worked there for thirty years. He was a newspaperman too. That's how I got started. Wanted to be just like my old man. Anyway, I was out on the street with a lot of other newspaper people. There weren't enough jobs on the other dailies to go around. Then a few years later, *Chicago Today* folds. Then the *Daily News* goes under. You couldn't buy a newspaper job here. I got a couple offers from out of town, but I didn't want to work the late desk in Podunk. So I went to work for a detective agency. I thought my skills as an investigative reporter might be useful. They liked me at first, then I started having trouble."

"What kind of trouble?"

"I didn't like some of the things I had to do and I told them. So they fired me. By then I had a wife and two little kids. I'd been with the agency long enough to qualify for my own P.I. license, so I went into business for myself."

"Are you happier now working for yourself?"

"A little, but it's not ecstasy." I said. I sipped my drink. "Now let me ask you something. Tell me about your father's girlfriend."

"Rita Baronette? I can't stand her. She's a hypocrite. And a greedy little bitch. She took Daddy for a fortune."

"Did they live together?"

"No, she has her own place."

"Does she have a key to your father's apartment?"

"I doubt it very much. Daddy was a nut about his privacy. He told me never to come to his place without calling first."

"How long were Rita and your father together?"

"About four years. But I don't think he really cared for her."

"Did he leave her some money?"

"I hope not. You'll have to ask her."

"Does she work?"

"She manages some kind of showroom in the Merchandise Mart."

"Did your father have other women on the side when he was going with Rita?"

"He did," Tina said. "Many."

"Is Rita the jealous type?"

"Very."

"Did your father and Rita have arguments?"

"Only one. It started when they met, and ended when he died."

"What did they argue about?"

"What a man and his mistress always argue about."

"What?"

"Everything. Who's going to do the dishes. I don't know."

"You say your father didn't love Rita?"

"I don't see how, she was such a bitch. He had no intention of getting married again, and of course he played around quite a bit. Rita wasn't too happy about that, and they fought over it constantly. She had wanted to be the next Mrs. Nockerman."

"And Mr. Nockerman wanted to be a happy bachelor. How many other girlfriends did he have?"

Tina shrugged. "I have no idea, and I don't know any of them, although I've met a few over the years. Are they suspects?"

"Possibly. By the way, did your father ever mention a man named W. Mayne Angler?"

She frowned. "No. Who is he?"

"Some guy from Chicago who was murdered a couple of days ago in Albuquerque. Worked for a clearinghouse here. I thought your father might've known him. They were both murdered the same way. Maybe with the same gun. I have a hunch Angler was hiding out. Maybe he was running from the same guy who killed your father."

"Seems he didn't run fast enough," she said.

"Or far enough. Can we go to your father's place after lunch?"

"Okay," she said, not too eagerly. For a moment she got that faraway, childlike look in her eyes again, the look of a sad little girl without a daddy. And just as quickly it was gone.

"Is it absolutely necessary to go to Daddy's?"

"Yes."

"Then let's have one more drink before we leave."

"Good idea."

12

Nockerman's apartment building was a glass-and-steel tower on the Outer Drive along the lakefront near Navy Pier. All the amenities were contained within it: shops, restaurants, health spa, an indoor pool, doctors and dentists, even a psychiatrist. You could spend your whole life here and never have to go out.

We parked in the subterranean garage in the tenants' area and Tina accompanied me while I reconnoitered around. I wanted to see if I could figure a way for someone to get from the garage into the lobby, up to Nockerman's place, and back out again without being noticed. Or if it was possible to slip in through the garage and take the service elevator up and down again. It wouldn't be easy, security seemed tight, someone was bound to see you—if they weren't loaded or asleep, or paid to look the other way.

Tina unlocked the door to her father's apartment and led me silently through room after spacious room, each with a broad view of the lake. Museum-quality paintings hung on the walls. I'd seen their cousins in the Art Institute and MOMA in New York. Each successive chamber contained lavish furniture and exquisite artistic appointments. There were massive Spanish antiques of vermiculated oak, an Italian Renaissance library table, a five-paneled Ming dynasty screen of black lacquer and inlaid mother of pearl. Obviously Nocky had a great love for fine things.

We came at last to a room at the end of a long corridor.

Tina pushed open the door and stood at the portal without entering.

"This is what you wanted to see," she said. "The room where Daddy was killed."

I looked into a large library/study, the entire wall to my left given over to bookshelves filled with volumes to the ceiling. The other wall housed an electronic amusement center, with state-of-the art stereo, tape deck, video recorder, stacks of video game cartridges and movies, and a huge TV screen.

"Right there," she pointed. "That's where I found him. Lying next to his desk." Her voice was small and tight, way back in her throat.

I walked past her and into the room, across a bare parquet floor.

"There was a beautiful Oriental rug in here," she said. "I sent it out to be cleaned."

I looked at her. "Before the cops examined it?"

"Of course not. They vacuumed it, took their samples, the whole bit. I sent it out a couple days later. Nothing unusual in that, is there?"

"No, I guess not."

I glanced at the floor where Nockerman had lain when Tina discovered him. The black leather executive swivel chair where he sat must have been turned slightly to the right, away from the desk, when the shot had been fired into his head. I looked to the far wall just below the shelves of electronic equipment and saw the hole where the slug had entered. On the floor beneath the hole were small flakes of white plaster, produced no doubt by the evidence technician who had dug out the lead.

I turned around. Tina had come into the room and was standing against the wall just inside the doorway, arms folded, watching me, apparently reluctant to enter any farther.

"Where was your father when you found him?"

"On the floor by the desk."

"Was he faceup or down?"

She started crying softly.

"I'm sorry, Tina, I've got to ask."

"He was faceup. On his back. His legs were crumpled beneath him."

"He probably slumped forward, his chair rolled backward, and he fell."

She shrugged, a slight doleful lift of her shoulders as if to say: What's the difference, he's dead.

"Do you mind if I take a look at his desk?"

"Go ahead," she said. "You won't find anything. The cops have been there already."

I turned back to Nockerman's desk, a long slab of black marble with legs of polished chromium. It was a massive piece of furniture set before a huge window overlooking the lake.

I rummaged through the drawers, foraging for something useful. There were mountains of the usual rubbish. I gave it all a cursory look. There was nothing of interest.

"What did the cops take away?" I asked.

"A personal check book, a Rolodex full of phone numbers, other odds and ends."

"Is there a safe here?"

"Yes, behind those books over there."

"Show me."

She walked quickly across the room and shoved some thick volumes aside on a lower shelf in the bookcase. "Here," she said.

"Did you find it open or locked?"

"It was locked, and empty when I opened it for the cops."

The safe was a Morgan and Edwards steel cannister, changeable combination, fireproof, about a foot and a half deep with an eight-inch inside diameter, top and bottom compartments. Not terribly big for a wealthy man with lots of valuables, but spacious enough to hold large amounts of cash.

"Who else besides you has the combination?"

"Just me."

"What's usually in that safe?"

"I don't know. Money, probably."

"Does your father have a safety deposit box?"

"Yes, downtown." She mentioned the name of a LaSalle Street bank.

"What does he keep in it?"

"Stocks, bonds, CDs."

"Anything else?"

"No, I just looked through it all last week."

"Did your father have any servants?"

"He had a housekeeper, a Japanese man who was a marvelous cook. He cleaned too. That's a rare combination. He was on vacation all last month. If he had been here that night, maybe Daddy wouldn't be dead."

Yeah, I thought, or maybe they'd both be dead. "What's the man's name, and where is he now?"

"Jimmy Mitsui. He's living in some hotel on Wilson Avenue near Sheridan Road. Just temporarily until he finds another job. I'm letting him use my name as a reference."

"I want to talk to him," I said.

"I'll give you his address."

"Is there a guest room here?"

"Down the hall."

"Let's take a look."

The guest room was handsomely decorated and rather simple: a tightly made queen-size bed, dresser, writing table, and nightstand. The walls were covered with contemporary lithographs, matted, framed, and glassed.

"I'm going to sell all the art," Tina said. "I'm consigning the whole lot to Sotheby's for auction. Maybe I'll keep one or two of the smaller pieces, but the rest of it goes."

I opened the sliding doors to the guest room closet and looked inside. There was a woman's quilted robe draped over a hanger, and a pair of silk pajamas on the upper shelf.

"They're mine," Tina said. "From the last time I stayed over."

"Who else stays over?"

"Nobody, as far as I know. Not even Daddy's girlfriends. He might have some woman up here for a quiet dinner once in a while, but when the evening was over, she'd go home. They'd never spend the whole night here together."

"How do you know?"

"Daddy told me."

"Strange behavior, isn't it? He wines and dines a beautiful young woman, makes love to her later, and then in the wee small hours he gets out of bed and drives her home?"

"He sends them home in a cab. He didn't like to wake up in his bed with some casual acquaintance."

"What about his regular girlfriend? He send her home too?"

"Sometimes she'd stay the whole night. But not always."

"Suppose your father had a visitor from out of town. Would he put him up here?"

"Definitely not. Daddy did not like overnight guests."

"Your mother ever stay here?"

"I don't think so."

I ambled around the misnamed guest room, systematically opening every drawer, looking for evidence that someone other than Tina had occupied it. I found none. I went into the adjoining bathroom, picked up a half-used tube of toothpaste, held it aloft for Tina to examine through the open door. "This yours?"

"Yes."

I opened the medicine cabinet. It was loaded with the usual crap. "All this stuff yours too?"

"It is," she sighed wearily.

I went back into the guest room. Tina was sitting on the bed, legs crossed, looking up at me.

I stood over her, hands in my trouser pockets. She smiled. It felt like an invitation. I smiled back. "Did your father hire someone part-time to fill in for the houseboy when he went on vacation?"

She frowned. "No, Daddy wouldn't trust a stranger in the apartment. When Jimmy was gone, Daddy took care of himself."

"Did Jimmy have a key to the apartment?"

"Yes. He gave it back to me when he left."

"And he knew the digital code for the security system?"

"Yes, of course. He had to let himself in and out of the apartment without setting off the alarm."

"Did you trust him?"

"Daddy did."

"Let's take a look at his room," I said.

Jimmy's room was immaculate, bare as a cloister, just large enough to contain a small bed, dresser, nightstand, and chair.

"Not exactly luxurious," I said.

"Jimmy is a simple man. He's a Buddhist, actually. Daddy offered him the other bedroom, but he preferred to live here."

I took a quick, perfunctory look around. Aside from the furniture, the place was empty.

"How did he react when he heard about your father?"

"He got a little shook up, but not hysterical."

"How many years did he work for your father?"

"Four or five."

"Did they get along with each other?"

"Perfectly. They left one another alone. Jimmy was very formal and proper. Daddy never got too familiar with him."

"They ever have any arguments about wages or vacation time, or anything else along those lines?"

"Jimmy argue with Daddy? Very unlikely."

"Did Jimmy ever have any visitors?"

"Never."

"Any nasty habits? Gambling, dope, women, the markets? Anything that might require large sums of money?"

"I don't know, Mr. Wolf. Daddy never talked to me about Jimmy."

"All right," I said. "Let's go see your father's bedroom."

As I examined Nockerman's bedroom, Tina remained in the doorway, as if not wanting to intrude upon this private place.

Nockerman's imperial-sized bed dominated the room. A huge, shaggy fur was flung carelessly across it for cover. Beneath the lavish animal pelt the silk sheets were wrinkled and rumpled, unchanged since Nockerman last lay upon them. The walk-in closet was thick with clothing—suits, jackets, silk shirts of every color hung on the racks in great profusion. I thought of Gatsby and his penchant for finery. There were mirrors everywhere, built into the ceiling over the bed, in sliding panels at the closet, angled on both sides to enwrap the viewer, covering part of a wall at the far side of the room. It was a chamber fit for Narcissus; in almost every corner his image would reverberate endlessly in the silvered glass. The bathroom was equally opulent: a large, resonant vault of brown tile, with sunken tubs, a bidet, Jacuzzi, sauna, Doric columns of ersatz marble, more mirrors, a gridwork floor of terra-cotta slabs, and erotic frescoes on the walls depicting Roman patricians and their nubile slaves at play. I was reminded of the sumptuous baths of emperor Antoninus.

"Find anything interesting?" Tina asked when I had finished looking around.

"Not much. Your father seems like a man who enjoyed very much what he enjoyed."

"I'm like that myself," she said.

Then she came slowly, tentatively into the bedroom. She wandered about aimlessly for a moment as if lost, picked up objects from the dresser to examine them briefly, glanced at herself in a mirror as she passed it, jabbed at her hair. At last she came to Nockerman's enormous bed and opened the cabinet doors on the adjacent nightstand.

"Look," she said. "Daddy's control panel. Radio, phonograph, television, VCR. Music, movies. See on the wall opposite the bed? There's a video screen. And look, there's a mini-refrigerator here, with an ice maker. Everything you'd need for a party."

She pressed a button on the console and music suddenly issued in soft, rich sound from concealed speakers. She hummed along for a bar or two, then as if angry, she punched a button on the panel and the drapes noisily parted from before the floor-to-ceiling windows. The room was instantly suffused with the cold, almost shadowless light that emanates from an overcast sky in late afternoon. Tina looked around quickly as if startled, surprised perhaps that the mysteries of this private place had suddenly dissolved when exposed to daylight. Then she fell sobbing upon the unmade bed, embracing the pillow as if it were human flesh and had the power to console her. I went to her side and stood over her as she curled, almost by reflex it seemed, into the fetal crescent; she looked so small and childlike you'd hardly guess she was a tall, full-bodied woman.

I put my hand on her shoulder, felt the sobs ripple through her body. "Go ahead," I said, "cry."

But I thought her crying jag was a bit excessive, especially so long after her father's death. Maybe it was even a little theatrical. Then I thought: it's me—I'm so cynical and corrupt, so conditioned by previous experience, I can't recognize honest human emotion anymore.

When I got home late that night my foot was hurting. I turned on the radio, found some jazz of the bebop era, closed my eyes, and leaned back on the couch. They say that sound has the power to heal. The universe hums: *ohm*. Yogis utter the same sound as a means of meditation, to calm themselves, as a physical sedative, mental purgative. The value of this practice has been confirmed by medical science: it can lower blood pressure, slow the heart rate, stop the flow of stomach acid. But the music on the box was a bit frantic, Bird and Diz in a horn wrestling match, melodic but combative. I poured myself a double Jack Daniel's in case the sound treatment failed.

13

Early the following day I went to Jimmy Mitsui's hotel in uptown. Tina had telephoned him to arrange the meeting.

Some of the worst hotels have the fanciest names and the most ornate facades. The entrance to the Hotel Magnifico looked like a mini-Alhambra, with spiraling pillars and Moorish arches of imitation marble, once a creamy white, now a dirty, weathered gray. The place may have been fashionable in the 1930s, but now it was strictly for welfare residents, hasty assignations, or to hole up with a bottle or a needle or something for your nose. The desk clerk, a huge mass of androgynous flesh, rang Jimmy and announced me.

The self-service elevator lurched and creaked to the sixth floor. I walked down the long corridor to Jimmy's room through a fog of noxious odors. He met me at his door, a thin, short man between forty and sixty, flat features against an ovoid face.

His room was a tiny cubicle with a solitary window. Laminations of paint flaked away from the jaundice-colored walls. There was a large stain across half the ceiling, seepage from the roof.

Jimmy sat on the edge of his bed in an undershirt, chino pants, and sandals over white socks. "This is just temporary," he told me. "I'm waiting to hear from the agency. They've got some job prospects lined up for me. Miss Tina gave me excellent references."

There was an open can of diet Pepsi on the window sill. In the wastebasket was a Kentucky Fried Chicken tub, filled with bones and crumpled napkins. On the dresser was a recent issue of the *National Enquirer*.

I sat on a wooden folding chair, reclining somewhat, arms folded across my chest, silent, watching, just waiting to see what he would offer without my asking, an old interrogator's trick. We looked at each other. Moments passed. Finally, he said, "I've already recited it all to the cops." There was something not quite polite in his voice.

"Would you mind telling me, too, please?"

"Let's see your license," he said.

I showed him my P.I. ticket.

"Makes no difference," he said. "The cops put me through a lot of shit, and I don't want to talk about it anymore."

"Got any idea who killed your boss?"

"Did you hear me, Wolf? I'm not answering any questions."

"I thought you liked Mr. Nockerman," I said.

"Barely. Now, adios."

"Just two or three questions and I'll go."

"You born in this country, Wolf? You don't savvy the language too well."

"Help me a little and I'll be out of here pronto."

"No," Jimmy said.

"Miss Nockerman says you and her father had some violent arguments lately."

"That's bullshit."

"You saying Miss Nockerman's a liar?"

"I'm saying you are. Because it never happened, and Miss Tina wouldn't lie."

"You ever have guests up? Women?"

"Mr. Nockerman didn't allow that."

"Yeah, but what about when he was gone?"

"You asking me did I do it behind his back?"

I nodded. "Yeah."

"Like all us sneaky Japs?"

"I didn't say that, Jimmy. I'm just asking if you did something perfectly human."

"Look, Wolf, Mr. Nockerman and I got along fine. No arguments over wages, and I never burnt the toast. He paid me well, and was very generous with the benefits. No, I don't know who would want to kill him. And yes, it's one hell of a coincidence that he got murdered when I was on vacation. But I was planning this trip for months. Los Angeles. I've got four sons there. I go every year at this time."

"What kind of life did Nockerman live?"

"He was out a lot, but when he was home things were quiet. He didn't entertain much."

"He ever do business at home?"

"Once in a while."

"Who came up? You ever catch a name?"

"I don't remember."

"What about the women he slept with? Who were they?"

"I just opened the door, hung up the coats, and served the drinks. I didn't know any of them."

"What about Rita Baronette? You ever hear her fighting with Nockerman about anything?"

"They were always fighting," he said dully.

"About what?"

"Nockerman's other broads. Miss Baronette didn't like that very much."

"Did you answer the phone when Nockerman was home?"

"Yes."

"You screened the calls?"

"I asked who was calling, yes."

"Did a guy named W. Mayne Angler ever call?"

Jimmy thought for a moment. "Yeah. Angler. I remember. First time he called he gave his real name. Later he used another name, but I recognized his voice."

"What name did he use?"

"Mr. White."

"When did he first start calling?"

"Six, seven years ago."

"Did he phone often?"

"Frequently."

"When was the last time?" I persisted.

"Just before I left on vacation."

"Did he ever visit Nockerman?"

"I think so," he said. "But I never saw him."

"He was murdered a couple days ago in Albuquerque."

Jimmy reacted with a slow blink and silence.

"You been back to Nockerman's apartment since the murder?"

"Just to pick up my stuff and clear out."

"Notice anything different about the place?"

"Yeah, a lot of people had been there besides the cops."

"How do you know?"

"Because the pillows on the couch in the den were all messed up. Mr. Nockerman never sits on the couch. He either sits at his desk or in the easy chair."

"You'd make a great dick, Jimmy."

"I'm not flattered," he said.

14

I drove to my office through relatively light traffic. In the mail were the usual bills and throwaways. As I dialed Duffy at Area One Homicide, I heard the noise and felt the thump of Dr. Lee's martial arts students flinging each other to the floor in the rooms adjacent to mine.

Duffy came on and I told him I talked to Jimmy Mitsui.

"Nockerman's houseboy? What did you get, Frank?"

"Did he mention Angler when your people talked to him?"

"Angler?" Duffy seemed surprised. "They guy you asked me about who got shot in Albuquerque? No, he didn't."

"I'm going to give you something, Duffy. But you're going to owe me a big one."

"Like hell I will. You can't withhold evidence in a criminal case. Come on, Wolf, what have you got?"

"Angler and Nockerman knew each other. Jimmy screened Nockerman's phone calls. He told me Angler phoned frequently but never gave his right name. He called himself Mr. White. Years ago, the first time Angler telephoned, he used his real name. Just that once, and never again. But Jimmy remembered his voice. So whenever Angler called, Jimmy made him."

"Did he ever see him with Nockerman?"

"He says no."

"So what is the connection here?"

"Nockerman was a commodity broker, Angler worked for a commodity clearinghouse. Maybe they were business associates?"

"Maybe they were just friends."

"I don't think so," I said.

"Why not?"

"Nockerman was a LaSalle Street high-roller. Angler was a computer technician. They weren't likely to hang out together. Got to be a business connection."

"It makes sense," Duffy said. "But why would Angler use a phony name?"

"He must have been misbehaving," I said. "Dd you ever run that Nockerman-Angler ballistics check?"

There was a moment of silence before he answered.

"As a matter of fact, we did. The gun that killed Angler appears to be the same one that killed Nockerman."

"So why the phony surprise when I mentioned Angler's name?"

He chuckled. "I like to fish. Sue me."

"So Jimmy did tell you about Angler?"

"Yeah, sure," Duffy said. "But he gave us what he gave you: nothing."

"Nothing?" Now I chuckled.

"Look, Wolf, I'd love to chat, but I'm tied up until my retirement. If you get anything I should know about this Nockerman-Angler thing, call me."

I had a momentary impulse to tell him about the ballbusters who stomped me, but I didn't mention it. At this point Duffy would just get in my way.

"Me find something before the Chicago Police Department? Is that some kind of joke?"

15

I'm an addict; I gamble to get high. With the sense of risk comes the rush that produces the exhilaration, the distortions of reason and perception. The brain gets loaded on a substance of its own manufacture.

I sat in my office, feet upon the desk, browsing through the *Racing Form*. I checked out the entries at Arlington Park, looking for any overlay, a horse with longer odds than its chances of winning would warrant. I found an interesting stallion in the feature that day, strong workouts, last two races wins going away, and a smart jock up that I really liked. It was a two to one favorite in the morning line. But the horse would probably close at shorter odds, maybe even money or four to five. It looked like a can't-miss, so I called Freedo to get six hundred down to win, all my poker winnings. One of his clerks answered the phone and took the bet.

Next, I telephoned Angler's widow, told her who I was, and asked if I could visit her that afternoon to ask a few questions. She agreed if I would promise to be brief.

She lived in a northern suburb just beyond the city limits in a modest brick ranch house, one of a whole block full of architectural variations on the same theme. I found the address and parked in the narrow blacktop driveway. In the back, where the garage should have been, was a heap of charred ruins. The fire, it seemed, had been fairly recent.

We sat in Mrs. Angler's living room in large upholstered chairs, a coffee table between us. The drapes were drawn shut, giving the place a funereal mood. Mrs. Angler wore a white blouse and blue denim jeans, the kind that look prehistoric even when they're brand-new. She was fiftyish, a hair shorter than medium height, a little overweight, and with too much makeup applied to conceal her black eye and the iridescent green-and-purple bruises on her face. Otherwise, she was rather pretty.

"Did you know my husband?" she asked.

"No."

"He was an artist. A genius."

"I wasn't aware of that."

She nodded. "Yes. Computers."

"What was his relationship with Mr. Nockerman?"

"Mr. Nockerman was his broker. Mayne made a lot of money in the last few years speculating in commodities. Mr. Nockerman advised him. We bought this house on market profits. And of course, Mayne used a lot of the money to update his computer center. He always bought the latest state-of-the-art equipment, no matter what it cost."

"Were your husband and Mr. Nockerman friends?"

"I doubt it. We never sent each other a Christmas card."

"Were you and Mr. Angler getting along?"

She uttered a brief, rueful laugh. "All you people ask the same questions, like you're reading from the same script. Yes, my husband and I loved one another dearly. Married thirty-two years next November."

"What happened to you?"

"This?" She raised her hand to her left cheek, touched the bruise gingerly with her fingertips. "A man came to the house the evening Mayne left town. He wanted to know where Mayne went."

Tears welled in her eyes. Her voice fell to a half-whisper. "It's my fault Mayne is dead."

"Back up a little. What happened earlier that day?"

"Mayne came home about four. He looked deathly pale, he was shaking, his voice was funny. He said he was in terrible trouble and had to leave town right away and hide. He'd explain everything later, he told me. It was a matter of life and death, he said. He made me promise to leave, too, that same day. He said I should go to my sister's place in Milwaukee, and eventually he'd contact me there. Don't pack, don't dawdle, just go, he said. I was scared as hell. I begged to come with him. No, too dangerous, he said. Then he grabbed me by the shoulders—I'll never forget it—'Someone wants to kill me,' he said. Who? Why? I was crying, hysterical. Who wanted to kill him? He said he'd tell me everything later. Then he threw a few things in a bag and said good-bye.

"I pleaded with him to tell me where he was going. He promised to get in touch. He made me swear not to call the police. Then he kissed me, and left."

She looked away, crying again. Then she turned back to me, continuing, her voice clear and steady.

"I suppose I should've called the police," she said, "even though Mayne told me not to. For years you lead a quiet, uneventful life. Then, suddenly, in ten minutes everything is changed. I was stunned. I just stood in the doorway like a statue, looking down the empty street. I don't know how long I stood there. Then I realized it was dark. I ran to the den to get our important papers—bank books, insurance policies. I started packing, stuffing clothes into a suitcase. But it was too late. There was a man in my bedroom. He was standing over me. 'Where's your husband?' he asked."

"What did he look like?" I asked.

"Ugly. His face was full of pockmarks. Dark, penetrating eyes, like a lunatic. Tall, stocky, with black hair. Maybe forty or forty-five. Very well dressed." She shuddered in horror at the memory.

" 'I've got an important message for your husband,' he said. 'Give it to me,' I told him. 'I'll deliver it.' 'No,' he said, 'it's for Mayne's ears only.' 'He went to Europe,' I said. 'On business. It was rather sudden,' I said. 'I don't know where he'll be staying. He's going to be traveling a lot. He said he'd call me in a week or two.' The man started slapping me around, screaming 'Where the hell is Mayne?' I swore I didn't know. He pulled a gun. My heart was beating like crazy. I thought I was going to faint. He shoved the gun against my head. He asked me again about Mayne. I was sobbing. 'Honest to God, mister,' I said, 'I don't know where he went.' I suppose I convinced him, because he left. 'Course, two days later Mayne was dead. And that ugly bastard probably killed him."

"Was the man alone?"

"I didn't see anyone else."

"Did you get a look at his car?"

"No. I just heard him drive away. For a long time after he left I didn't move from the bedroom."

"Did you ever see him before?"

"No."

"Could you identify him if you saw him again?"

"Absolutely. I'll never forget that face."

"What did you do after he left?"

"I finished packing, got in my car, and drove to my sister's place in Milwaukee."

"Were you followed?"

"I don't know," she said. "I wasn't paying attention."

"Why didn't you call the police?"

"I told you, Mayne made me promise. Besides, I thought maybe he *had* committed some kind of crime."

"What kind of crime?"

"I don't know. I wasn't thinking straight."

"Your husband ever commit a crime before?"

"He didn't seem the type. But now I wonder. How do you think that man found my husband?"

"Maybe he followed you to your sister's house, and patched into the phone line. Did your husband telephone you there?"

"Yes."

"And you phoned him in Albuquerque?"

"Yes," she said.

I was silent.

"So it's my fault he found Mayne?"

"I don't think so," I said. I didn't want to send her on a long-distance guilt trip. "They were probably watching the airports, spotted your husband, and tailed him to Albuquerque."

"You really think so?"

"Absolutely. Now, tell me what was in the garage that someone wanted destroyed."

"Just Mayne's computer equipment. Terminals, monitors, high-speed laser printer, modem, the whole works. All destroyed. We lost all our business and investment records too."

"No back-up files?"

"I told him more than once to make copies, but he never did. He was always busy in there. Locked himself in like a hermit."

"What did he use the modem for?"

"To send and receive data from other computers. Or to access the clearinghouse computer to work at home."

"Some people use a modem illegally," I said.

"Yes," she said, "to steal information."

"Or destroy it," I said. "What was your husband's job at the clearinghouse?"

"Assistant director of computer operations. A very important position, but he should've had the top job. Mayne knew everything about computers. But his bosses were jealous of his ability, so they never promoted him."

"That your analysis or his?"

"His, but I agreed once he told me the facts."

"Why didn't he quit? He had enough money."

"Money was beside the point. He enjoyed the work."

"Thanks for your help, Mrs. Angler," I said. "Can I see your husband's garage now?"

"Go look," she said. "It's nothing but an ash heap."

I poked around for a while in the ruins of what was once Angler's garage computer center but found only grotesque agglomerations of molten plastic and charred rubble. Whatever information he might have kept here was lost forever, along with his high-tech hardware and software. I wondered if Angler's computer could pick horses.

I drove back to my office, called Freedo and got the bad news: my horse had run out of the money. Adios to my poker winnings, and good-bye symmetry.

In view of the recent beating I took, I thought it would be prudent to run a test on the homemade alarm system I kept under my desk. I telephoned my pal Hershey, the guy who owns the corner deli. His name is really Harry, but he's a chocoholic, always munching on fudge, brownies, or a candy bar.

"You never call me unless you need something," he said. "What is it, you want I should cater a bar mitzvah for you? Loan you money? Reserve you a table for a party of twelve? What?"

"Hershey, I'm pressing the button here. You getting my signal?"

"No light on this end, your batteries must be dead."

"Or the rats ate my wire," I said.

I made a note to get new batteries and check out the connection. I had a powerful hunch I might have to use it soon.

When I got home later that night I examined my injured foot. The bruise was black, blue, and green, like the iridescent body of a fly. I sat on the floor in the living room in the lotus position, meditating, sending *prana,* the life force, to my damaged extremity, a Yoga trick I had learned from a former lover of mine. If you do it right, the procedure eliminates pain and promotes tranquility. I had a bottle of Jack Daniel's handy in case it didn't work.

16

I was in bed when the call came sometime after midnight. It was Tina.

"I'm sorry, Frank, I know it's late, but I'm—I'm at Daddy's place. Can you come over?"

"Are you all right?"

"I need to talk, Frank. Please."

"I'll be there in half an hour."

There was hardly a light on in the apartment, yet even in the dark I could see Tina's eyes were red and swollen from crying.

"God, I'm so glad you came, Frank. I've been here all day, going through Daddy's things. I've got to get rid of the clothes, the furniture, everything. I thought I might give it all to the Salvation Army. Then I got very depressed. I needed to be with someone. Don't be angry at me for calling you."

"I'm not angry, Tina."

She led me into Nockerman's bedroom. The dimmer had been turned way down. There was a strange, sweet odor in the room.

"What's that smell, Tina?"

"Daddy's cologne. I accidentally broke the bottle."

She turned up the dimmer, flooding the bedroom with light.

"Look, Frank." She gestured toward Nockerman's closet. The mirrored doors had been shoved back and the cavernous space where Nockerman had hung his clothing was wide open.

"It's all yours, Frank. Take it."

Hanging there was a fortune in expensive clothing—suits in every fabric and cut, sport jackets, blazers, trousers, shoes, and the rainbow of silk shirts that had made me think of Gatsby.

"I want you to have Daddy's clothes, Frank. They'll fit you perfectly."

I walked silently into the closet and ran my hand slowly across the suits, feeling the smooth silks and gabardines, the rough tweeds, the heavy wools and flannels. My fingertips tingled against the varied textures. Then I stepped back, and out.

"Thanks, Tina, but I can't."

"Please, Frank. Otherwise I'll give it all to the Salvation Army."

"I appreciate this, Tina, but I don't want any of it."

"Give me one good reason."

"I'm superstitious."

She blinked, glaring at me in disbelief. "That's crazy."

"I know."

"All right." Disappointed, she turned and walked away.

"I'm exhausted," she said then, kicking off her shoes and lying down on her father's bed. Reaching over to the nightstand console, she turned down the lights. "Come lie here next to me."

"Tina—"

"Believe me, Frank," she interrupted, "I have no intention of seducing you, so don't say something that'll make you look ridiculous."

"It's late. Let's go. Unless you intend to sleep here."

Abruptly, angrily, she got up from the bed. "All right, let's go."

"You too tired to drive?" I asked. "I'll take you home."

"No, I'm okay."

We walked quickly through the dark apartment to the front door and left. As the elevator dropped swiftly down to the subterranean garage, she apologized again for calling me so late at night and asking me to come to her.

"It was selfish of me to call and wake you."

"Forget it," I said.

"But why'd you come over in the middle of the night if you didn't want to see me?"

"Strictly business."

She smiled knowingly. "Really? Okay. You sure you don't want my father's suits?"

"I'm sure."

"Then tomorrow out they go, to the Salvation Army. There's going to be some well-dressed homeless people, size 40 regular." She chuckled.

As she got in her car, she told me, "I wish I wasn't so wiped out. I'd let you take me somewhere interesting. I'll call you." And she drove away, up the ramp and out.

I knew I shouldn't have come when she called. As the diplomats say, it sent the wrong signal. She was right to be pissed when I declined her invitation to join her in bed. Driving back home I pondered my ability to resist any such future invitations.

On my way to the office, I picked up a light breakfast to go, the morning papers, and a *Racing Form*. I sipped coffee and telephoned Mrs. Nockerman. For several days I'd been leaving messages on her answering machine for her to call me, but I never heard from her. I wanted to ask her some additional questions about Nockerman's friends and business associates.

I opened the *Racing Form* and took a quick look. There was a filly in the third at Arlington who made me some money last year. She was stepping way down in class to run in a low-end claimer, so I called Freedo and bet the horse six hundred across the board.

"What do I owe you now, Freedo?"

"Six hundred; you drop this one it's twelve hundred."

"Tonight you'll owe me," I said.

"Don't hold your breath."

I phoned Mrs. Nockerman again and left another message. So I decided to go to the Merchandise Mart to see Rita Baronette, Nockerman's girlfriend. She was not there. I was told that Ms. Baronette had left her job recently and now usually spent her days at the East Bank Club.

I drove to the East Bank Club between Illinois and Kinzie streets on the north branch of the Chicago River, and parked in the underground garage. My ancient, dusty Chevy looked like a recently excavated fossil among all the pricey new foreign jobs with their high-gloss finishes and vanity plates. The East Bank Club: the in place to meet, eat, play, and sweat, with an Olympic-size pool, Jacuzzis, hot tubs, restaurants, bars, tennis and racquetball facilities, an indoor track, Nautilus equipment, sleeping rooms, and pervading it all the lush fragrance of coed carnality.

I climbed three flights up the atrium stairway, past the glass-enclosed workout rooms where the highly motivated inflicted unspeakable tortures upon themselves in the name of vanity, health, and good sex.

I went out onto the roof and threaded my way slowly through a virtual carpet of almost-naked human bodies. They lolled and reclined like a herd of seals basking upon the sun-warmed rocks along some desolate Pacific Beach—with the Chicago skyline for a backdrop. In the midst of this mosaic of flesh was a small outdoor bar, and I stopped to ask the bartender, a tall, jock type, swarthy and surly with black curly hair and drooping Zapata mustache, if he knew Rita Baronette.

"Yeah, I know her," said Mr. Hunk.

"Is she here today?"

"Over there," he said, pointing a well-muscled finger. "The zaftig one in the blue bikini."

"Thanks," I said, and ambled away through the horizontal crowds. I was beginning to sweat and felt like a pariah in my suit and tie among so much bare skin.

Rita Baronette appeared to be snoozing; her eyes were closed and her breathing was deep and regular. I stood over her for a moment, admiring her beauty and mature body, ample in its volumes, graceful in its curves, but neither fat nor flabby. She was thirty-five or thereabouts, with dense, dark-brown hair worn short and feathered.

"Goddamnit, you're in my sun," she suddenly barked in a brutal Chicago twang. She sat up, squinting. "Who the hell are you?"

"Frank Wolf. I'm a private investigator. I've been hired by Mr. Nockerman's ex-wife to look into his murder. Please accept my condolences," I added dryly.

"I'm sorry. I thought you were trying to pick me up. Sit down, Mr. Wolf. I knew you'd show up sooner or later. I had heard that Abel's ex hired you."

I took off my jacket, opened my collar, and took off my tie. She sat up on her lounger and moved her legs to give me room. I sat at her feet, facing her.

"What can you tell me," I asked, "that might be useful?"

"I loved him very much. He was an extraordinary man. He had guts and character and a knack for living. I have no idea who'd want to kill him. Or why. Unless it had something to do with his business, or with—" She stopped in mid-sentence.

"Or with what?" I asked.

"Never mind," she said. "It's too far out."

"What?"

"Nothing. Forget it."

"Rita," I said, without a trace of anything hostile or in-quisitorial in my voice, "you and I are on the same side in this thing."

She smiled. "You look hot. Would you like a drink?"

"Later," I said. "After we've talked."

"All right," she said. "I was going to say that maybe Abel's killing had something to do with dope."

"Dope?"

"Abel used a little coke now and then. Maybe that has something to do with his murder."

Abel Nockerman a snowbird? I wasn't much surprised. Over the years certain hot-shot trader-types had been busted for using or dealing.

"This dope angle is new to me," I said. "Did you mention it to the cops?"

"Actually, no. I didn't think it was important."

"Not important?"

She shrugged.

"Do you use it yourself?"

"I have a toot on occasion. For recreational purposes." She watched me closely for my reaction.

"Was Nockerman just a user?"

"What do you mean *just* a user?"

"Did he sell it too?"

"Abel sell coke? What the hell for? He had all the money he'd ever need."

"Didn't he ever sell an ounce or two to his friends?"

"No," she said emphatically, then added, with a little less certainty, "not that I know of."

"Then why do you think his murder is dope-related?"

"I don't think that at all. It was an idea that crossed my mind—a lousy idea, I can see that now."

"It doesn't make sense to me either. If there's a dope connection in Nockerman's murder, then he may have been more than just an occasional user. Who'd he buy it from?"

"I don't know. I never asked."

"Did he buy a lot at a time?"

"I don't know, but he always had plenty."

"You never saw who he bought it from?"

"No."

"He ever mention any names or locations when he talked about buying?"

"He never talked about buying."

"Didn't he ever tell you where he was going to score, or drop someone's name, or tell you someone was bringing the coke to the house?"

"He never said anything."

"Was he a heavy user?"

"He was a weekender, like me. It never hurt him. He worked, he played tennis, he went skiing, he did everything. No ill effects."

"Did he use it openly with his friends, or did he only get high in private?"

"He was fairly private about it, although he wasn't opposed to a little snort at some social affair."

"So his friends were aware of his coke habit?"

"Look, Wolf, it wasn't a habit. He used it for recreation, like a lot of people."

"But his friends knew he used?"

"Abel didn't have many friends. He wasn't the kind of man who gets close to people."

"You and he were pretty close, weren't you?"

"Come on, gimme a break."

"I heard you quit your job."

She shifted positions on the recliner. "Yes, Abel left me some money. We were together five years, and I never asked him for a dime. Anyway, Abel bought some insurance, a small term policy—for my protection, he said. I told him I didn't want it, but he insisted. That's the kind of man he was. Very generous."

"How much did he leave you?"

"Believe me, I'm not set for life—unless I live very modestly. Sure, Abel bought me a condo, a car, clothing, even jewelry, but no way am I independent. Not even with the insurance money sitting in CDs."

"How'd you feel about Abel's other girlfriends?"

"What other girlfriends?"

"What he had on the side while he was going with you. Tina told me about them."

"Oh, *those* girlfriends. I never met any of them."

"Did you and Abel argue about them?"

"I argued, Abel didn't. I could've killed him. Is that what you're looking for? Yes, I got so mad and jealous, I could've murdered him. But I didn't."

"Did you have a key to his place?"

"No. I went by invitation only."

"Why weren't you with him that night?"

"I was sick."

"With what?"

"Stomach flu. I stayed home."

"Can you prove it?"

"What do you want? A stool sample?"

I laughed. "You're funny," I said.

I was starting to sweat through my shirt, a growing dark-blue stain against the lighter blue of the broadcloth. I waved over a cruising waiter and ordered a gin and tonic. Rita asked for a diet 7-Up with lots of ice. In the dark eastern sky far out over the lake a thunderstorm was roiling. I heard it growl and rumble as it slouched toward the city, smelled its freshness on the erratic breeze.

"Would you like to change into a suit and go for a swim?" Rita asked me.

"I'd love to," I said.

"Well?"

"I can't. I'm working today."

"So take off a few hours. You'll dock yourself."

"I'm naturally lazy. You give in to that once or twice, gets to be a habit. Thing like that could ruin a man."

She chuckled. "Is that your elaborate way of saying no?"

"Yes."

The drinks were brought and I paid the waiter.

"Health and success," I said. We touched glasses and drank.

"Rita," I said, "did you ever see Abel with a tall, ugly, dark-haired man with a face full of pockmarks?"

She looked skyward for a moment. "Yeah, I think I know who you mean. Looks like a monkey, but always well dressed?"

"Face like Swiss cheese?"

"Yeah, that's him. Who is he?"

"I don't know yet. Where'd you see him?"

"Abel knew him. He used to sit with us once in a while at the racetrack. Arlington, the club house. Abel had a box there. Or sometimes I'd be driving around with Abel and he'd stop somewhere, get out of the car, and the guy would be there, waiting. They met like that several times."

"What's the man's name?"

"I don't remember. In fact, now that you mention it, I don't recall Abel ever introducing us."

"Do you remember where Abel used to meet him?"

"Usually on the Near North Side, the Rush Street area."

"Would you recognize the guy if you saw him again?"

"Would I have to identify him in court or something? I'd hate to be wrong about somebody."

"Slow down, Rita, you're getting way ahead of yourself. What makes you think he's going to jail?"

"You think he killed Abel, don't you?"

"How'd you figure that?"

"Am I right?"

"That's a definite maybe."

I finished my drink and stood. "Thanks, Rita, you've been very helpful. If you think of anything else, give me a call." I handed her my card.

"You're leaving already?"

"You got more to tell me?"

"Not about Abel. I loved him, but life goes on."

"So it does. By the way, sooner or later the cops will be back to talk to you again. They may not be as cordial as the first time."

"Why not?"

"You neglected to tell them that Abel used coke. They're not going to be happy about that."

"What'll I do?" She didn't seem terribly concerned.

"When the cops ask why you didn't mention the dope, tell them you forgot, then cooperate fully. Or take the fifth and say nothing. Just be sure to clean up your condo in case you get surprise visitors with search warrants. I wouldn't worry too much about it—the cops don't want you. But if they find a little flake stashed under your bed, they'll have you at a slight disadvantage."

As I left it was starting to rain. The rooftop crowds were hastily picking themselves up and scattering to the exits. The wind rose and the air turned cool.

18

I drove back to my office through a torrential downpour. Traffic lurched and skidded on the wet asphalt. With my windows shut and air conditioner busted, the inside of my car turned steamy. Visibility zero. I rolled the window down a crack. Gusts of rain blew in along with the backwash of cars speeding blindly through puddles.

There was no place to park near the office, so I was forced to leave the car more than two blocks away. I ran through the streets without an umbrella, drenched to the skin. I stopped at Hershey's for the papers and a large coffee to go.

Back in my office I took everything off and laid my clothing out over chairs to dry. I sat naked and opened the newspaper to the sports pages, looking for something to get me even. The Cubs would be starting a long home stand tomorrow, fresh off nine straight wins on the road. They'd open against the Braves, losers of their last six. So with the Braves in a slump, and Chicago hot, there'd be some cinch money here. I called Freedo's to make a bet. The man himself answered the phone.

"Frankie, boy, how are you? You ain't been around lately. It ain't because you owe me twelve hundred, is it?"

"No, just been busy. What's the line on the Cubs game tomorrow?"

"Cubs eight–seven over the Braves."

Which meant I had to bet eight bucks to make five. The bookie quotes odds to the number five. In this case, if you bet the favorite you lay eight to five. If you bet the underdog, they lay you seven to five.

"I'll take the Cubs for eight hundred," I said.

"Eight hundred on one goddamn ballgame?"

"Will you take my action or do I find another book?"

"Okay, you got it. Cubs eight hundred to win."

"Cubs win I owe you seven hundred."

"That's right, Frankie. And if you're wrong you're in for two grand. Good luck."

About four o'clock Tina called.

"I'm afraid I wasn't very good company last night," she said. "I'm sorry. I'll be better tonight. You can take me to dinner. Pick me up in front of my gallery at six-thirty."

Like most P.I.s I had my rule about not socializing with clients or members of their families. It gets in the way of business, people get hurt, sometimes even the P.I.

"I've got a previous engagement," I said.

"I want to talk about Daddy, Frank. I've got more to tell you."

Maybe she did have more to tell me about her late father, but why did it have to be that night over dinner?

"Will you pick me up, Frank?" she said. I heard in her voice the need to be with someone.

"All right. I'll be there."

19

By the time I met Tina that evening the rain had stopped.

We drove along Sheridan Road into the suburbs, past mile after mile of the incalculable wealth of the fabled North Shore. Here upon the stunted bluffs along the lakefront stood the huge mansions that proclaimed the success and power of the men who had built them.

"Where are you taking me?" Tina asked.

"Highwood," I said. "I know a first-rate Italian restaurant there."

"I hope they make good martinis."

She leaned over, reached up, and grabbed the rearview mirror to turn it toward her.

"How do I look?" she asked, studying her face, poking at her hair. "Am I a mess? I had a terrible day."

She pushed the mirror away and I readjusted it.

"You look great," I assured her. "What happened?"

"I was hanging a new show at the gallery today. The artist drove me crazy. First he said the lighting wasn't right. Then he bitched that I set his prices too low. God, what a pain in the ass. You'll meet him at the opening. I do expect you to come, you know."

"Where's your mother been lately? I've been trying to get her on the phone."

"She went to Europe. This thing with Daddy upset her quite a bit, much more than she let on. She needs a long rest. The police were through with her, so she left."

"Went to Europe? Jesus Christ. Why didn't you tell me?

How'm I going to conduct this investigation with your mother out of the country? I've got questions to ask her."

"You can ask them when she comes back," Tina said. "Meanwhile, I'll be giving you your weekly check."

"Where is she? I want to call her."

"She made me swear not to tell a soul where she went."

"That's going to make things very difficult," I said. "Tina . . . did you know your father used cocaine?"

For a long moment she stared at me. Silent.

"Yes, I knew," she said at last.

"Why didn't you tell me?"

"I was afraid."

"Of what?"

"I don't know. Maybe I just didn't want the whole world to know my father was a doper. And maybe I didn't want the police snooping around in his life because they'd find out things about him that I wouldn't like."

"What things?"

"Nothing, I don't know. I'm just saying *maybe* . . ."

"So you didn't tell the cops?"

"No."

"They probably know anyway. They must've found drugs in the house and figured it out."

"Maybe not," she said. "Before the cops came I went through Daddy's apartment, found the coke, and flushed it down the toilet."

Rather a cold-blooded act for a shocked and grieving daughter, I thought. She discovers her father's body, then has the presence of mind to clean things up a bit before the cops come. That was something to think about.

"I didn't call the cops right away," she said, as if she had read my mind. "At first I was too stunned to do anything. I just sat on the floor near Daddy. I don't know how long I sat there. Finally, about dawn, just before I telephoned the cops, I found his stuff and got rid of it."

"How much coke did he have?"

"A big plastic bag full."

"I take it your mother knew about this and didn't tell the cops either?"

"Yes."

"Why not? Her reasons the same as yours?"

"More or less."

"You both concealed evidence from the cops. You and your mother. Could be some nasty feedback if the cops find out. If they ever talk to you about your father using coke, tell them it's news to you. That goes for your mother too."

The restaurant was packed and there was a waiting line, but I had called ahead and reserved a table and we were seated immediately. We ordered martinis on the rocks and veal scaloppine for the both of us. We ate slowly, chatting about everything but her father's murder. As we lingered over coffee and amaretto she asked, "Why isn't a man like you married?"

"I was once. I thought I told you."

"You mentioned it. What happened?"

I shrugged, signaled silently that I didn't want to talk about it. She got the message.

"What about your kids?" she asked.

"Boy and a girl. Ten and eight. I love them both very much. I see 'em once, twice a year. My ex comes back to visit her folks every summer. So I pick up the kids and take 'em to an amusement park or maybe to a ballgame. Some winters I fly out to L.A. for a long weekend and see 'em again."

"Were you a faithful husband?"

"Yeah, I believe in fidelity. 'Course, once we were separated and the divorce proceedings started—well, I don't believe in celibacy. I heard it's unhealthy. Causes headaches."

She smiled. "Have you been in love since your divorce, Frank?"

"No," I said. "I don't fall in love easily."

20

We drove back to Chicago under clear skies and brilliant moonlight. We chatted amiably about nothing for a few minutes, then we fell silent for miles on end as we wound through the deep ravines and lazy curves on Sheridan Road and listened to jazz on FM radio. I felt no compelling reason to talk, or ask questions. Tina gazed out the window for long stretches, turning occasionally to look at me as if about to say something. Then without speaking she'd return to her unremarked observation of the passing scenery.

Once we neared Chicago, and the traffic got heavier and faster, we started talking again, as if inspired by the adrenaline rush that comes with hazardous driving.

"Let's go to my place tonight," she said. "You've never been there."

"Where do you live?"

"In the Hancock."

The Hancock was an aborted obelisk of one hundred stories, ending abruptly before coming to a point.

I drove into the parking entrance and up the narrow spiral ramp, ascending floor after floor like a corkscrew, my car just missing the concrete sides as it wheeled around the endlessly climbing curve. I caught glimpses of the city through the open spaces in the wall.

I parked on the twelfth floor and took the elevator with Tina up to her place on eighty-nine.

The view from her apartment made me dizzy for a moment; I had the sensation of floating over the city.

"Overwhelming, isn't it?" Tina said. "Daddy bought me the place."

She must have loved her daddy very much, maybe too much, perhaps even obsessively, considering the abundance of photographs of the late, lamented Nockerman scattered about. A dozen or so blown-up photos of Tina and her father together hung on the walls in aluminum frames. Two more large studio portraits of Nockerman were enclosed by elaborate baroque gilt frames and sat side by side on an end table next to the couch. There was even a series of photos of Nockerman as an impoverished urchin on the streets of westside Chicago, and then somewhat later as an enterprising and better dressed teenager in Rogers Park. But there was no photograph anywhere of Tina's mother, not even a small Polaroid, nor a group photo of the happy family together.

"I don't see any pictures of your mother," I said.

"I have one in the bedroom," she said. "Want a drink?"

"Not now."

"Stay with me tonight, Frank," she whispered.

"Yes."

We were standing at the floor-to-ceiling windows, looking out over the city. She turned and kissed me on the lips. I tasted her lipstick, smelled the rich fragrance of her hair. Then, without a word, she led me by the hand to her bedroom. We kissed again, the soft sibilance of our breathing amplified in the semidarkness. Then she broke gently from my embrace and whispered, "I'll be right back."

In the dim light of the nightstand lamp I saw her come naked out of the bathroom. She moved silently toward me, her nudity reflected to infinity in the great wall of mirrors behind her. Midway to the bed where I lay she stopped, smiled, extended her arms, then turned slowly so that I might see and savor her beauty. It was a gesture so apparently free of inhibition I thought she might have done it before, more than once.

She was exquisite, the volumes and contours of her body like classical sculpture made flesh. Her breasts were large, mature, but with the coral-colored nipples of a woman who has never been pregnant, and even at a distance, with my hands not upon them, I could feel their satisfying heft. I could feel all of her, in fact—so powerful was her physical presence.

As I watched her, I had that sense of apprehension that precedes sex for the first time with someone new.

Then, suddenly, she turned again, ran across the room and jumped into bed beside me, giggling like a mischievous child who has scampered naked through the living room as mother and father sat there entertaining the preacher and his wife.

Slowly, by degrees, our bodies warmed the sheets and we overcame our initial shyness. But there was something tentative, almost adolescent in her lovemaking, a suggestion of inexperience that surprised me. Because of the sensuality she radiated, I had expected her to be a more adept and avid lover. But she wasn't; maybe it was just first-time syndrome, the restraint she might feel with a near-stranger, even in bed.

We lay together on our backs in post-coital lethargy, our bare legs entwined, an airy goose-down comforter for cover. When the wind blew I heard the metallic creaking of the building.

"They say this building sways in the wind," she said.

"It bends or it breaks."

She ran her fingers over my body, slowly, carefully, like a blind woman reading a page of Braille, as if the topography of my flesh could disclose secrets of my character. Then she felt the deep scar at my abdomen, the narrow vertical line that bisects me from pubis to navel.

"What is this, Frank?"

"I was shot once. I thought I was going to die. I lay in the street bleeding to death and thought about things."

"What?"

"It made a believer out of me."

"A believer in what?"

"In life. How precious it is."

"Everybody knows that."

"No, they only think it. They don't know it. There's a big difference. You got to experience it."

"Tell me, Frank, why'd you get divorced?"

"I had a gambling problem. I was out of control. Just like my father. I owed every bookie and shylock in town. Their muscle kept coming to the house night and day to collect. Sometimes I couldn't even pay my phone bill or make car payments, or even the rent. I borrowed from everybody: friends, relatives, shylocks. I cashed all our insurance policies, hocked everything that wasn't nailed down. I'd gamble until I lost everything, then I'd go out and hustle more cash and start all over again. I was sick, I couldn't stop. Well, my wife couldn't stand living that way, and I couldn't blame her. So we got divorced. That shook me up real bad. She married again and moved to California with him and the kids."

"I'm sorry, Frank. I know how much you love your children. I hope they don't disappoint you, the way I disappointed Daddy. He had such high expectations for me."

"We're bigger disappointments to ourselves than to our fathers," I said.

"You really think so? I don't know. Daddy wanted me to be something special. Unfortunately, I'm just ordinary."

"By whose standards?"

"Mine," she said. "It's a feeling I've had all my life. You know something, Frank? I was sort of a gambler myself. For my twenty-first birthday, Daddy bought me my own seat on the Board of Trade. I was still a kid and there I was in the pits, a trader. I lost plenty that first year. Daddy just laughed it off and bailed me out. Mother was furious. One week I took a hit for almost ten thousand. Mother got word of it and went ape. 'Why do you hurt me this way, Tina?' Well, that's Mother, everyone's out to get her. Most of all me. She never did care for me. She's not my real mother, you know. She wasn't able to have children. I'm adopted."

"Adopted? I didn't know. You look so much alike."

"You live with people long enough you get to look like them. Sometimes you get to think like them. You even pick up their neuroses. Anyway, I don't see that much resemblance. My real father committed suicide. Shot himself. Money problems, they said. But it's never just money problems, is it? I was six at the time. I felt he deserted me. I loved him so much, and he went away without even saying goodbye. I suppose I never forgave him. I thought: why would he kill himself with such a lovable little girl in the house? His death certainly changed whatever notions I had about my own value in the scheme of things. A short time later my mother died too. She was an alcoholic. Drank herself to death. So in a sense both my parents were suicides."

She was quiet for a moment. Then, in a less reflective

voice she said, "Anyway, I was sent to an orphanage, and a few months later I was adopted by the Nockermans."

"Lucky," I said. "You were adopted by such a good family."

"Yeah," she said softly. "But when you're adopted, Frank, you always feel like you're on probation. I was the best-behaved little girl, I'd do anything to make my foster mother and father happy. I was deathly afraid of being deserted again. Then I started growing up and began to see what kind of a person my so-called mother really was. But I was crazy about Daddy. That's why I became a commodity trader. I thought it would please him."

"Why'd you stop trading?"

"I got interested in art. I wanted to open a gallery. Daddy helped me get started. But I still have my seat at the Board of Trade. Daddy said I should lease it out, make some money while I'm not using it. But I wanted to keep it for myself. Gives me a sense of independence to know I can walk into the pits any day I want and start trading. You can't understand that, Frank, unless you're a trader yourself. There's no thrill like it."

"So I've heard. But it's basically a crap game, isn't it?"

"Not if you know what you're doing."

"Meaning what?"

"Forget about charts, crop reports, supply-demand figures. You trade on the moment. Tick by tick. The market's alive—it breathes in, it breathes out. You dance with it. That's how Daddy traded. I just couldn't do it as well as he did."

"Why'd you quit?"

"I was losing too much money. I felt terrible about it. Daddy kept paying my losses, but he didn't seem to mind. At least he didn't say anything. But it ate me up. So I decided to get out. But God, it was a kick trading in the pits. Even when you're losing." She paused for a moment, then said, "Were you a disappointment to your father, too, Frank?"

"Probably not as much as I once thought I was. But who knows, he died so long ago. You get older, your view of things changes, especially the way you think about your parents. He wanted me to be a great newspaperman. Columnist, foreign correspondent. Something classy. He was a Chicago newspaper photographer more than forty years. Damn good one too. Nominated for a Pulitzer three, four times. Won every other prize around. But his personal life was a mess. He pissed away a fortune—gambling, women, fancy clothes. My mother and him kept separating and getting back together."

I leaned over to look at Tina. Her eyes were closed.

"I'm awake, Frank," she said. "Go ahead."

"My father gambled away everything he ever made. Chicago used to be wide open. Years ago, before Daley the First was elected. There were bookie joints and wire rooms all over the Loop. Huge places with chalkboards on the walls, long rows of caged windows like a bank. You could bet any track in the country, and some guy called the whole race over the loudspeaker. And I mean, these places were posh. Some of the biggest people came—city alderman, judges, show-business celebrities, cops in uniform. I saw it. My father used to take me when I was a kid. I'd have to sit there for hours sometimes while he'd make his bets. He'd get me a sandwich and a Coke, and I'd wait. So I figured it out—the men gambled, the little boys watched."

"You loved your daddy?" Tina asked, her voice drowsy.

"I idolized him. I wanted to be just like him."

"And he loved you?"

"Yeah."

"Were you close?"

"Very, at least when I was a kid. He took me with him everywhere. Weekends and vacations. I went with him on his news assignments all over the city. Police stations, criminal courts, baseball and football games, hockey, basketball, fires, auto wrecks, disasters—I saw it all. My dad had a four-by-five Speed Graphic with a flash. He'd shoot some event and a few hours later I'd see it in the pages of the *Scrutinizer*. With his credit line: Photographs by Dave Wolf. My father. I was real proud of that. I thought working for a newspaper was the most exciting, important, heroic thing a man could do."

"Why did this happen to us, Frank?"

"I don't know. Let's not analyze it."

"No, let's not. I've just always been attracted to strong, older men. Maybe some lack of strength and maturity in myself."

"Is that what Freud would say?"

"Freud's out of date. Frank . . ."

"What?"

"You've heard a lot of bad things about my father, haven't you?"

"Bad like what?"

"Just negative comments. Especially from my mother, and Daddy's colleagues, and maybe even from Rita. You understand why people say these things, don't you?"

"Tell me."

"Jealousy. The urge to destroy something more beautiful than themselves. If you hear ugly things about him, that's why. None of it is true, believe me."

"None of what is true, Tina?"

"I don't know, just the lies people make up. Promise you'll check with me first, Frank, before you believe anything nasty you hear about Daddy."

I promised.

21

The telephone was ringing when I got to the office the following morning. It was Duffy.

"You keep nice hours," he said. "It's after ten."

"That's what I like about working for myself."

"You still working on this Nockerman thing?"

"Yeah. Why?"

"Ever hear anything about a banker named Ervin Osvald?"

"No, who is he?"

"He was murdered a few days ago near Barstow, California. Single shot to the head with a high-caliber handgun. Just like Nockerman and Angler. Seems he was running or hiding. The bank he works for here reported him missing a few weeks ago, couple days after the Nockerman murder. Sheriff's police out there've been in touch with us. Ballistics got a match on the slug. Same gun that killed Nockerman and Angler. So, I thought maybe you'd know something about this Osvald."

"Nothing. This is the first I heard about him."

"Okay, then I'm giving you a new lead. Something develops, you call me. We're cooperating with Barstow on this."

"Spell Osvald for me."

Duffy spelled it out, and gave me the name of his bank.

"Thanks, Pat," I said. "I'll buy you a drink."

"A drink? Hell! A case. Tullamore Dew."

I hung up the phone and opened my newspaper to the sports pages. The Cubs had lost five to one. I owed Freedo two grand.

Physicists have postulated the existence of an infinite number of alternative universes in which all the permutations of possibility are realized. It's a great comfort to know that in another universe I'm rich, famous, and never lose a bet. Sounds dull as hell, but I'd like to try it for a while.

I leaned back in my reclining chair, propped my feet up on the desk, and began browsing through the long computer printout that Lane had given me of heavy losers among Nockerman's clients. Thirty-seven people were listed who had lost a hundred grand or more speculating in commodities with Nockerman's brokerage firm.

Chronic losers may sometimes have a passing impulse to blow away their bookies. Market players may occasionally feel the same way about their brokers. But seldom, if ever, are these murderous urges acted upon. So I didn't expect to find Nocky's killer among his high-rolling bustouts. The most I hoped for was a decent lead or two, a notion of how Nocky did business, and a glimpse perhaps of his elusive private life.

The champion loser among Nocky's clients was a guy named Harry Henley; net loss of five hundred and sixty-six thousand over the past few years. There were several other losers in the quarter-million-dollar range. The rest had lost from a hundred to more than two hundred grand. As a rule, losers don't talk about their losses. Nevertheless, I telephoned the top half dozen, explained my interest in their relationship with Nocky, and asked if they would see me to answer a few questions.

One was out of town. Another wouldn't talk about anything, period. A third threatened to sue me and Lane for invasion of privacy, and for violating the confidential broker-client relationship. Three others agreed to see me, including Henley.

He received me in his penthouse office atop the boxy high rise he owned on the south edge of the Loop. He sat behind a broad slab of white onyx eight feet long: his desk. It was totally bare except for a telephone console, yellow legal pad, and a gold mechanical pencil. At his back spread a vast panoramic window with a wide-angle view of the city to the north. On the walls were huge framed photographs and architect's drawings of Henley's real estate projects and developments. A long table on the far side of the immense room bore a scale model of what appeared to be some utopian vision of tomorrow's suburbia, complete with miniature shrubbery and trees around the houses, tiny automobiles, even minuscule street signs. The only thing missing was little people.

Henley came out from behind his desk, shook my hand vigorously, and looked me square in the eye with a salesman's sincerity. "I'm in real estate," he said. "Maybe you heard of me. My name's always in the papers. I got a P.R. firm does that for me. Have a seat. How about a drink—Scotch, coffee, diet soda? No? Suit yourself. Now, how can I help you, Mr. Wolf?"

He was short and beefy, early fifties, thick lips and a meatball nose, tan, balding, dressed in light-blue slacks and a white silk shirt wide open at the throat.

"I'd like to ask you some questions about Abel Nockerman," I said.

Henley returned to his desk, his huge leather chair hissing as he sat down.

"It's a goddamn shame what happened to Nocky," he said. "I spoke to him on the phone just a few days before he was killed."

"Did he say anything unusual?"

"Like what?"

"Like he was having business or personal problems?"

"Nocky wasn't the type to confide in people. The only thing we ever talked about was the markets. Or the economy. Maybe a little politics once in a while. Nothing ever deeper than that."

"So you weren't very close?"

"Me and Nocky? No way. I used to talk to that man every day, sometimes six and seven times a day when I was heavy into the market. But I can't say we were friendly."

"How did you and Nockerman get connected?"

"Nocky had a great reputation on the street. Excellent personal service and very good advice. And not only in commodities. Months before the stock market took that big fall, Nockerman advised me to sell all my equities. Said there was a big correction coming and I should liquidate my whole portfolio. But I didn't believe him. I thought he wanted me to sell my stocks so I'd have more money to put into commodities. With him. Anyway, I didn't sell, and I got hurt real bad. I should've listened to him."

"But his advice must have been lousy, considering all the money you lost."

"No, just the opposite. My first few years with Nocky were sensational. Remember that killer frost in Brazil, destroyed a third of the coffee crop? He tipped me to that, called me in the middle of the night. Buy coffee options, he told me, first thing in the morning when the market opens. I did, and made a quarter million. Then somehow Nocky got advance word of a Mexican peso devaluation. So he told me to short pesos. When the peso dropped a few weeks later I covered my short and made a huge profit. Then there was that revolution in Africa. I forget the name of the country. Government shuts down the copper mines for the duration. Nocky said get long in copper because world prices would skyrocket. So I bought copper futures. Made another bundle. Hell, Nocky made me money right and left in those days."

"So how come today you're such a large net loser?"

"Two reasons," he said. "Nocky's advice turned bad. And I began to think of myself as an expert because of all the money I made. I started trading on my own, picking 'em myself, trying to beat the odds. Nocky was still my broker, but he wasn't my advisor. I made a lot of bum trades. I threw good money after bad. I didn't know when to cut my losses. Sometime I'd have a winner, but I'd ride the bastard too high. Then the market would break, and I couldn't get out. A nice profit would turn into a goddamn loss. I don't care how much money a man has, that hurts. Then I started playing half-assed, just for the action. I'm the kind of guy always likes to have something going in the market. That was my big mistake. A man has to know when to walk away."

"When Nocky started passing out bum tips, did he start losing his clients?"

"I don't know. But I don't think it hurt his business. In fact, I heard he got even bigger."

I nodded. "And at the same time he continued to speculate in the market and his losses got heavier?"

"Exactly."

"Why'd he gamble away in the market the money he made as a broker?"

"You're asking me? Am I a shrink?"

"What would happen if Nockerman lost more money than he earned?"

"He'd have to make it up some way."

"How?"

"Borrow it, steal it, I don't know."

"Who's the well-dressed guy with the pockmarked face that Nockerman used to hang out with?"

"I have no idea who you're talking about."

"Did you know that Nockerman used cocaine?"

For an instant Henley seemed to lock in a freeze frame, breathless, blinkless, speechless. A split second later he thawed. "No, I wasn't aware of that." His voice was a little reedy and came from the back of his throat. "Expensive habit, isn't it?"

"You've tried it?"

"Me? Hey, I'm a real estate developer. Word gets out I'm doing coke, what happens to me at the banks? Who's going to loan money to a snowbird? You know what I'm saying?"

"I see your point."

I stood. He stood. "Thanks for your help, Mr. Henley." I handed him my card. "Just in case you need to call me for any reason."

"Would you like my opinion, Mr. Wolf?"

"Certainly."

"I think Nocky was killed by one of his lady friends."

"It's a possibility," I said. "Isn't *lady* a slang term for coke?"

Two other heavy losers both confirmed Henley's story about Nockerman's rise as a market advisor and speculator. And neither of the two could explain how Nocky's brokerage firm continued to flourish handling customer business during the long stretch when he couldn't pick a winner.

But one of them said something interesting, which gave me something new to think about.

"Why don't you talk to the winners, Wolf? Winners get pissed off, too, you know."

"They do? Why?"

"Maybe they didn't win enough. Maybe the broker tipped the IRS. Who knows? Some people are just crazy. They don't need an excuse to kill somebody. Win or lose, it doesn't matter."

22

A winner kill Nockerman? It seemed unlikely, tanta-mount to wasting the golden goose. I knew practically nothing of Nocky's relations with his clients, only what I had just been told by that trio of losers, and what I remembered from observing him some years ago.

I had sat in his office watching and listening as he tele-phoned at least a dozen clients, one after another, talking in that strange lingo of numbers, letters, acronyms peculiar to the business of commodity trading.

"We'll buy fifty Feb Comex gold. Write an MIT order ten dollars above the market, and take profits when there's an upswing. You'll have to put up margin money."

His voice was hoarse, as usual, but buoyant with opti-mism and self-confidence, qualities common to the best bro-kers and salesmen. He reclined in his swivel chair, feet on his desk, table-top calculator in his lap, unfolding a long computer printout as he talked. From time to time, he glanced my way, smiling at me with amusement, or winking, as if we shared some secret, or were coconspirators in some scam.

"You're up thirty-eight thousand on your cotton," he told some client. "Forty K up on your plywood. Gold closed down again today, made a triple bottom on the charts. It's ready to bounce. Let's sell the wood and cotton and get long in gold. When it starts to climb we'll run trailing stops. If it dips, we're out."

He used the collective *we* and *us,* no doubt to give his clients the impression he was with them in the markets and exposed to the same risks, rather than just a commission-house broker pushing product.

For almost an hour he spoke to client after client, not so much suggesting their market moves, nor advising them, but dictating what and how much they buy and sell.

"Whatever I tell 'em, Frank," he said to me, "they jump. You know how much I just made in commissions? You wouldn't believe me. I don't have to call these people, you know. I can manage their money however I want—they're all discretionary accounts. But I keep in touch. Makes 'em happy to hear from their broker. Makes 'em think they're on the inside. But hell, Frank, it's selling, not trading. I'd rather be in the pits."

I had been doing some investigative work for him, and I handed him the written report he wanted.

He set the file folder on his desk without looking at it.

"You know why I'm so good on the floor?" he asked me.

"Why?"

"Because I don't give a shit. I never trade scared. I ain't afraid of being broke. Wouldn't like it, but it wouldn't be the end of the world for me. Like it is for some guys. I seen people walk off the floor weeping. Complete bust-outs. Everything down the drain. Next thing you hear they blow their brains out. Not me. That's my edge. Plus, I got the balls. That's what really counts. When I first started in this business, I used to scalp. Make an eighth, a quarter point every trade. In, out, all day long. Small risks, small gains. You trade like that, why trade at all? There's nothing to it. No money, no kick."

"You got anything else for me to do?" I asked.

"Not right now. But you know, Frank, I'm surprised at you. I thought a guy like you'd go for the money. I remember you as a kid, always hustling a game—pool, poker, whatever. What'd they call you, again? Duke? I used to watch you dealin' stud on a blanket at Farwell Beach. All fuckin' day you'd sit there, people comin' and goin'. They'd bust out, get more cash, sit back in. You were how old, fifteen, sixteen? Playing horses, baseball, football cards, whatever fuckin' moved. That's why I thought you'd go for something with more money in it than the newspaper. What the hell can you make writin' for a newspaper? Unless you're Royko or somebody. Then you wind up as a P.I. It don't figure. You still gambling away your paychecks?"

"I'm trying to quit," I told him.

He laughed. "Not you, Frank. You get too much charge out of it. You ever play big-time poker? I played Hold 'Em against Stretch Pickett. World Series of poker in Vegas. Ten thousand dollar buy-in. Half-million payoff. What do I know from poker? Nothin'. But I wanted to play. So I bought a seat in the game. Stretch was at my table. Skinny, slow-movin' guy. Not much of a talker. You know what I saw when I looked in his eyes? The Grand Canyon. A big, empty space. The man's nothin' but a poker machine. You could hear his fuckin' brain click. That's what it takes. Anyway, I tapped-out in under two hours. But you know something? The fuckin' game's too slow. And it's too fuckin' quiet. I was bored. It ain't physical like trading. There's no kick to it. Gimme the pits any day. That's where the action is, Frank. In the pits. Nothin' else is real. I walk out on that floor, it's like combat. I feel like a *matador,* a killer. It's exhilarating. I love it."

23

Driving downtown to pick up Tina I got the news by radio: the Cubs had lost 3–2. Jesus Christ! It defies logic. I made the right bet. It's the goddamn Cubs. They're unlucky. They never catch a break. I had bet the Cubs two grand to win and now I owed Freedo four grand plus the Vig. *Okay, okay,* I thought, *I'll get even tomorrow.* The Cubs were pitching some hot new kid, already a six-game winner, and the season was only a couple months old. I'd call Freedo later tonight, get the line on tomorrow's game, and bet four Gs on the Cubs. A win would almost even me out.

I parked in the tow-away zone on Michigan Avenue in front of Tina's gallery. Traffic behind me honked and beeped. A bus swung around me spewing black diesel fumes. In the rearview mirror I saw a cabbie cursing me, probably in both Spanish and English. Tina was to meet me here at five sharp. It was already fifteen after. A cop in checkered cap and black leather jacket came striding toward me from across the street.

Then from the other direction Tina came running, coat-tails flying, long hair trailing in the blustery wind. She jumped into the car, slammed the door, and we were off, the cop shouting at us in our wake.

"Am I late?" Tina asked. "Let's grab a bite and go to your place. I've never been there and you've never asked me, so I'm inviting myself."

"Very gracious of you." I smiled.

"Thanks. I feel wonderful tonight. I finished most of the work for the opening today. The invitations went out. I

called all the critics and asked them to come. I sent out publicity releases, ordered the food and drinks, told Byron again
what a genius he was and not to worry. Now fill me in on
what you've been doing."

I told her about my interviews with Henley and the others.

"Were you aware that your father had lost a lot of money
speculating?" I asked her.

"Of course I was, Frank. Why don't we eat in Chinatown."

"You got a yen for Chinese?"

"Yeah, and a yen for you too."

"Likewise."

I found a parking space on Clark Street, just south of
the Chinatown gate near the On Leong building, an ornate,
three-story pagoda with red-tile roof, an alien architectural
presence among the other unremarkable brick buildings of
the neighborhood. Even at that early hour crowds of tourists
were already ambling up and down the sidewalks, window-
shopping or browsing through the Oriental trinketoriums
with their paper snakes and smiling plaster Buddhas. We
passed up the flashier restaurants with their blinking convo-
lutions of neon, decor of ersatz cinnabar and plastic bamboo.
Instead, we went to a favorite place of mine, a storefront
joint that looked more like an unpretentious luncheonette
than the best Szechuan eatery in the city.

The room was plain, packed and noisy, illuminated by
harsh fluorescent light from bare overhead fixtures, and
filled with the most luscious blend of aromas. We sat in the
back at a tiny table for two. I watched her as she studied the
menu. For a moment I wished she were someone else so I
could take her to bed guiltlessly, and without worrying about
the possible complications of our affair. At last she looked up
and smiled. "Are you staring at me, mister?"

"Yes, I am."

We ordered—Kung Pao Shrimp and shredded beef with
peppers and scallions. Waiting for our food to come I asked
her how she knew about her father's losses in the market.

"There were big arguments about it between him and
my mother. She wanted him to stop speculating. But he
wouldn't, or couldn't. You know about compulsive gambling.

It's a disease. People can't help themselves. My mother never understood that."

"Do you know roughly how much he lost?"

"I don't know exactly. Maybe close to a million, from what I heard around the house. I don't remember, it was too long ago."

The food came. We bent to our meals and ate for minutes on end without uttering a word, looking at one another across the table from beneath our brows in silent communion.

"How is it?" I asked her finally.

"Yummy. How's yours?"

I opened my mouth and breathed out loudly like a dragon exhaling flame. "Incendiary but delicious," I said.

"Give me a taste," she said.

"You'll burn your tongue."

"I don't care. I like hot things."

24

Once the sun goes down there's never a place to park near my apartment building. I drove around the block several times, scouting a crevice into which I might squeeze the old Chevy, but cars occupied every last centimeter of space. At last I gave up and parked next to a fire hydrant.

"You'll get a ticket," Tina told me.

"I'll write it off as a business expense."

"They won't allow it. This is a pleasure cruise."

"Not if we talk about the case."

"No more tonight, Frank, please."

"Okay."

I inhabited a small one-bedroom unit on the third floor of a three-story redbrick six-flat on North Greenview Avenue. The stairwell lights were out, so we climbed the three flights slowly and carefully, arms hooked, stumbling occasionally in the dark like a pair of drunks. I poked around blindly with my key for a few moments and finally opened the door.

"Turn on all the lights," Tina said. "I want to see everything."

I flicked on a table lamp. Tina stood in the center of my living room and did a 360-degree pan, taking it all in.

Here's what she saw: on the right, occupying the entire wall, floor-to-ceiling bookcases. On the bottom shelf was my stereo outfit, at opposite ends stood the speakers. Straight ahead was the small dining/kitchen area with the built-in cabinets and butcher-block table. To her left was the couch, six feet of bloated upholstery in burnt orange and an occasional cigarette hole from the days when I smoked. On either flank were end tables, one of which was piled high with books, magazines, newspapers, and an empty bag that once contained nachos. And finally, facing the couch obliquely from the far side of the room, was a large color TV squatting on a roll-out table.

"How long have you lived here?" Tina asked.

"Since my divorce."

"Not as squalid as I thought it would be."

"Thanks a lot. I think."

"I expected something else," she said.

"What? A place that would gag a hyena?"

"No," she chuckled, "just a bit more of a mess."

"Want a drink?"

"Do you have any white wine?"

"I'm fresh out. How about a Scotch?"

"Okay."

Tina browsed among my books while I went into the kitchen, poured two glasses of Johnnie Walker over rocks, and brought them back into the living room.

"You've got such interesting books," she said. "They say you can figure out a man's personality from what he reads."

"Don't believe it," I said, handing her a glass.

"Why all the books on astronomy?"

"Few years ago I got interested in ESP. Thought it might help me pick a winner. That led me to study meditation and Zen Buddhism. From Zen to particle physics, and from there to astronomy."

"All that just to get lucky?"

"Yeah. Obviously it didn't work. But I stayed interested in the universe."

She sipped her Scotch. "Do you ever feel unconnected, Frank?"

"Meaning what?"

"That you're not really connected to anything. That you're on the outside looking in at people with real lives and real emotions?"

"No, I never felt that way. Not even as a reporter. Life's always had me by the throat."

She drained the remainder of her drink in a single draft.

"Let's see where you sleep, Frank."

25

For breakfast I scrambled a huge batch of eggs, toasted some English muffins, poured full tumblers of orange juice, and brewed a pot of strong coffee. We sat at the table in my minuscule dining room. Brilliant early-morning sunlight flooded in through the windows. Tina looked marvelous, freshly showered, subtly scented and wide awake.

"You look great for a girl who didn't bring an overnight bag," I told her.

"You'd be surprised what I have in my purse," she said. "Say, do you have any chili peppers or Tabasco?"

I found a bottle of Tabasco in the cupboard and set it on the table. She splashed it generously over her eggs.

"I want to ask you a few more questions about your father."

"Frank, you're hopeless. We just spent the night together. It's Saturday morning, the sun is shining, and there you sit playing private eye again."

"Okay, you've made your point. I'll take you to the Cubs game today."

"No, I hate baseball."

"How about a drive in the country?"

"Fine, we'll have a picnic."

"Great. But will you answer some questions first?"

"Now I know why they call you guys gumshoes."

"Was there a change in your lifestyle as a result of your father's losses? Economy measures, belt-tightening?"

"If there was, I didn't notice."

"Because he was still making plenty of money on his brokerage business?"

"I guess."

"Or maybe in some other business?" I prodded.

"Like what?"

"I don't know. I'm just trying to figure how a man who lost a million kept living so well."

"Maybe his losses didn't hurt him that much."

"Do you have your father's books from this period?"

"They're at his office. On the computer."

"I'd like to take a look, Tina."

"Sure," she said. "I'll call Teddy. He'll help you find what you want."

"You sure?"

"Certainly. Why do you ask?"

"He didn't exactly weep with joy last time he saw me."

"No? I can't imagine why not."

"I can, if he's been stealing from your father. Come with me when I go there. He might be more cooperative if I show up with his boss."

"I won't be his boss much longer. I don't think I mentioned it—Teddy's going to buy Daddy's company."

"Where'd he get the money?"

"He's got partners."

"Who?"

"I don't know. The rich, silent type. He made an offer a couple days ago."

"Why didn't you tell me?"

"It never occurred to me."

"I've got to know everything that pertains to your father. Business dealings, private life, all of it."

"Okay, Frank. No problem."

26

Teddy was not delighted to see us when we showed up at Nockerman's office unannounced. He unlocked the door and admitted us with barely concealed irritation. His eyes were weary and unfocused from staring too long at columns of figures.

"Nice to see you, Tina," he said without a smile. He looked at me then, shoved his thumbs into vest pockets and nodded curtly. "Hello, Wolf."

"Mr. Wolf and I are going to look at some records," Tina said. Something cold and authoritative in her voice reminded me of her mother.

"They're in your father's office. On the computer," Teddy said. "You know how to work everything?"

"Yes," Tina said.

"Fine," Lane said. "Help yourself."

"I want to talk to you later, Teddy," I said.

"I'll be here."

We went into Nockerman's private office, a large room flooded with light from windows that gave on LaSalle Street. In front of the windows was Nockerman's desk, a Federal period original in dark oak, loaded with the usual rubbish, including a Quotron monitor with keyboard for accessing market prices. There was also a large, framed color photograph of Tina, age about eighteen or so. To the left of Nockerman's desk was a Reuters commodity news service wire. To the right on a small table was his computer outfit.

Tina pulled up her father's large, reclining desk chair and sat down at the computer keyboard. I carried over a desk chair and sat down next to her. She turned on the system, searched through the library and selected a disk, then shoved it into a slot to the right of the VDT.

"I'm going back nine years," she said, her eyes on the monitor. "That's the year before Daddy and Mom were divorced, the year he started losing heavily in the market."

I watched a montage of computerized documents flash upon the screen in rapid sequence as she hit the keyboard: tax returns, invoices and paid bills, checking account balances.

"This is all Daddy's personal stuff. The business stuff is on different disks. Look, here's his market profit-and-loss statements. Year by year. Daddy kept such good records. He was great with numbers. To me it's boring. I'd rather be in the pits."

She scrolled through the monthly P&L data. Nockerman, in effect, was his own client. Each trade of his was listed, the date, amount, and price of every purchase and sale, with a running tally on his net dollar position. There were several winning trades here and there, but the majority were losers. He had dropped more than half a million before his divorce.

I said, "Let's see how his business went after the divorce."

She searched through the archive, found the appropriate disk, shoved it into the system and called up the annual balance sheets. Year after year, according to the data, despite Nocky's heavy losses speculating, his brokerage firm made huge profits.

My eyes were starting to burn and my head ached from too much green computer screen. I've heard these machines can trigger an epileptic seizure, maybe even cause mental disorientation. Such is the price of its efficient, uncomplaining, inexhaustible servitude.

"One more thing before we turn it off," I said. "Get last year's client field and see who made money in the market."

Tina inserted a new disk, somewhat impatient, it seemed to me, to conclude our lengthy record viewing.

I asked her to punch up Angler's account.

I spelled out the name, she typed it in, hit another key or two, and Angler's account came up on the screen.

"He's a position trader," she said. "Not a guy who's in

and out of the market every day. He buys something, holds it, then months later sells it at a profit."

"What's it mean?"

"Your Mr. Angler is very sharp, or he's been getting great advice from Daddy—probably the latter. He usually sells out near the top of a market. Not an easy thing to do. And he holds things long enough for the minimum capital tax bite."

"How much did he make last year?"

"Three hundred and thirty-two thousand in profitable trades. Is this the man who was murdered recently? The man you think was killed by the same person who killed Daddy?"

"Yes. Now let's see what you got on Ervin Osvald, if anything."

I spelled it, she tapped it out, and there it was: Osvald was also a Nockerman client. I was not surprised.

"You say Osvald was also murdered?" Tina asked.

I nodded.

"Mr. Osvald is just like Mr. Angler," Tina said, "a position trader. Last year he made three hundred thousand. He must have been advised by Daddy, or very lucky."

"Maybe he was too lucky."

"What do you mean, Frank?"

"I believe in luck, but not in epidemics like this. These people had some kind of edge."

"Like what?"

"I don't know yet. Ask the computer to print out a list of all clients who've won two hundred grand or more during the past ten years."

She entered the command and the printer started noisily rolling out the list of winners. I stood over the machine and watched. There was Angler near the top of the list. Net profit over nine hundred grand. The machine kept printing —Nockerman's profit a staggering seven million, five; Osvald, one million, six. There were others, but I turned away.

"Amazing how these people beat the market," I said.

I looked at the printout once more and noticed another Nockerman—Ruth J., with winnings that totaled more than two million.

"Here's a surprise. Your mother's name."

"I know," Tina said. "Daddy gave her tips on the market, even after the divorce."

I tore the long sheet from the printer. and handed it to Tina. "Take a look. You know anyone else on this list?"

She scrutinized the printout, humming a monotonous tune. Then she suddenly stopped. "Teddy?"

I looked at the paper over her shoulder. There it was: Theodore H. Lane. Net profit over the past several years: nine hundred twenty thousand and change.

"Is this *our* Teddy Lane?" I asked.

"Same address, same phone number."

"I thought he was just a working stiff. Let's go ask him how he got so lucky."

27

We came out of Nockerman's private office and found Lane sitting hunched over his desk in the anteroom, energetically fingering a large calculator.

"Let's talk, Teddy," I said.

Without lifting his head or losing a beat on his keypad he muttered, "In a minute."

"Want some coffee?" Tina asked me. "There's a machine in the outer office."

"Good idea."

"Would you like some coffee, Teddy?" Tina asked Lane. No response.

Tina shrugged and left the room. I sat down in a chair across the desk from Lane. "I never realized you were such a wealthy man," I told him.

He looked up from his labors, mouth open, apparently still in the trance induced by high finance. "Huh?"

"How'd you make all that money in the market? Nockerman advise you?"

"Yeah. How'd you find out?"

"I ran a computer check on Nocky's clients."

Lane blinked, said nothing.

"Two Nockerman clients were murdered," I said. "Then there's Nocky himself, also a murder victim. What's the connection between them, besides the obvious? You got any ideas?"

"Who else was murdered? Who are you talking about?"

"Angler and Osvald."

"Oh, yeah, I know who they are," Lane said. "I read

about it in the papers. They've got substantial equity in their trading accounts. I'll be closing them out soon as I get official word from the estates."

"Did you know Angler and Osvald personally?" I asked.

"They were Nockerman's clients. He brought them into the house. Angler, I didn't know at all. But I knew Osvald. We used his bank for company business."

"What kind of business?" I asked.

"We had deposits there, customer funds, checking accounts."

"So Nockerman's banker was also his client?"

"Anything wrong with that?"

"You tell me."

"There's nothing to tell."

"Banks don't normally approve of their officers playing the market," I said. "Did Osvald's superiors know about his speculating?"

"If they did, there was no fuss about it. And if they didn't, what's the difference?"

"No difference at all, I suppose, if he wasn't stealing from his own bank to finance his gambling."

"That's the bank's problem, not mine."

I nodded agreement. "It's a dangerous business," I said, "being a Nockerman client, especially if you've made a lot of money. Mrs. Nockerman's on that list. I'm worried about her. And then there's you, Teddy. You were also a Nockerman client who made a small fortune in commodities. Maybe you should have police protection. I can arrange that for you if you'd like."

"Don't bother. It's not necessary."

"What did you do with all the money you made?"

"That's between me and the IRS."

"You were a pretty big shooter for a guy just working for wages. Where'd you get the money?"

"Nocky loaned it to me. I didn't even ask him. He just saw something real solid, told me I should get on it, and offered to loan me the cash."

"Nocky was a generous man, wasn't he?"

"Damn generous," he said. "He did the same thing for a lot of people."

"Who?"

"I don't remember offhand, but there were plenty."

"I hear you're buying the firm."

"Yeah, that's right."

"Using your own money."

"Some of mine, some of my partners'."

"Who are your partners?"

"Just a couple of guys looking to invest."

"Want to tell me their names?"

"They prefer to remain anonymous."

"Why?"

"Goddamn it, Wolf, I don't know. And besides, it's none of your fucking business. It's my business. And it's private."

"Hey, Teddy, don't get a hernia. I'm just asking."

"I don't like this goddamn third degree."

Tina came back in. "We're out of coffee." She sat down next to me.

I asked Lane, "Will Mrs. Nockerman remain with the house as your client?"

He glanced for an instant at Tina, then looked at me again. "I'd be happy to serve as Mrs. Nockerman's broker."

"Yeah, yeah, I'm sure you would. But have you and she talked about it?"

"We haven't, no. It's possible we may never do business at all. I think she only played the market when Nockerman gave her a tip. That's right, isn't it, Tina?"

"I wouldn't know," Tina said. "Mother never discussed business with me."

Without taking my eyes from Lane, I said, "Tina, when are you going to run a full-scale audit on this place?"

Lane stared back at me, blinking slowly like a frog.

"I've already done it," Tina said. "To establish value for the sale."

"Find anything funny?" I asked.

"No, nothing."

"Do you trust me *now*, Wolf?" Lane asked.

"Should I? You didn't tell me some things you should've."

"Like what?"

"Like how much money you made speculating. Like Angler and Osvald had been Nockerman's clients. And like who are your new partners."

"All that's confidential information. Why should I mention any of it?"

"Because you want to help me find Nockerman's killer."

I wanted to ask Lane a few more questions about the amazing winning streak of Nocky and his clients, which defied all the laws of probability. But, of course, I couldn't ask the necessary questions with Tina sitting beside me—questions which, by implication, would impugn the integrity of her late, lamented, and obsessively loved father.

I got up and told Lane, "I promised Tina we'd go on a picnic today. I'll be back to see you next week. When will the sale of the firm be concluded?"

"End of the month," he said.

"Well," I said, "I hope you'll have Nockerman's luck. In the market, I mean."

28

It was a beautiful day to drive out to the country.

We stopped briefly at a downtown deli and bought a pound of corned beef, sliced rye bread with seeds, mustard, large juicy dill pickles, potato chips, a six-pack of 7-Up, fudge brownies, and a big package of paper napkins. And then we fled like fugitives, heading north into the cool, peaceful sanctuary beyond the city.

We rounded the sharp S-curve near the Baha'i Temple and I turned the car left onto one of the quiet residential streets and found a place to park. Dodging traffic, we ran back across the hot asphalt of Sheridan Road, me with arms full of paper bags, Tina with the rolled-up blanket I keep in the car. A moment later we felt the cool, soft, tree-shaded grass of Wilmette Beach Park beneath our feet.

I spread the blanket out upon the sand near the water. Tina and I unpacked the groceries, then kicked off our shoes and peeled away our socks to run hand in hand barefoot along the beach, the breaking waves licking at our ankles. We laughed, splashing through the spume, the water drenching us and much colder than I thought it would be. To our backs the wind shoved us along until for a brief moment or two as I ran I had a sensation that birds must feel an instant before they become airborne.

Breathless and laughing, we returned to our blanket and collapsed. We were starved, our appetites sharpened by the outdoors, and so we consumed vast amounts of food and drink until we were fully requited. She rolled up her jacket

to provide a pillow for her head and lay down, sighing, grati-
fied. I sat down beside her, yawned, only half-resisting an
urge to stretch out and nap.

A cluster of low clouds scudded across the fathomless
sky of pure cerulean blue, flogged by a sharp northeast wind
bearing the tang of lake water dense with life. As we talked
our voices were lofted away into the air, the sound dissipat-
ing among the shrieking gulls.

I wanted to ask her more questions, but I checked the
impulse. The day was too beautiful, and there was plenty of
time to ask on the way home.

We stayed for the rest of the day, chatting as we lay on
the sand, or falling into long silences as we looked out upon
the ever-changing colors of the restless lake.

We left late that afternoon, driving back to Chicago in a
clear, amber twilight.

As we passed that stretch of Sheridan Road with the
lake on one side and Calvary Cemetery on the other, I said,
"Something bothers me."

"After a day like this?" she asked.

"Just one or two things . . . How much of your father's
business did Lane know?"

"Everything. They were inseparable. Especially when
Daddy was just getting started in the early years. They even
spent their vacations together. They went to Florida one
year. I remember now, there was an accident. They had
chartered a boat. Daddy, Teddy, and a client they got
friendly with. I think they were all involved in some kind of
business deal too. The man's name was Arcana. They were
all on this boat and suddenly one of those tropical storms
came up. The boat almost sank. Daddy and Teddy were all
right, thank God, but the man with them was washed overboard."

Just as I had told Duffy. I remembered reading about it
at the time in the local papers. I had never given it a second
thought, except to ponder the lucky break that spared Nockerman and Lane, but which swept Arcana into the ocean.
Nocky had brought back the damaged boat, a small motor
launch apparently unfit for the heavy winds and rough seas
of a mid-summer storm off the Florida coast. The inquest
ruled Arcana's death accidental. I remembered thinking at
the time that it was only coincidence that just a few months

earlier, Nocky had me check out Arcana for Outfit connections.

"I know your father was an honest man," I began cautiously, "but his long winning streak in the market was incredible. Odds don't favor a run like that, no matter what the game."

She answered blandly, "Sometimes it goes that way. Is that what's bothering you?"

"Not exactly. I'm just wondering if your father might have been in on some market fix. That would explain why he consistently made so much money."

"Daddy fix the market? It's not that easy. The market's too big. It's probably easier to fix a horse race."

"But suppose it could be done. Didn't some superrich Texans corner the soybean market a few years ago?"

"That's not fixing the market."

"But it's influencing prices."

"Daddy was too little; he didn't have enough money."

"But maybe he was the brains behind some bigger people who did have enough money."

"You're suggesting Daddy was crooked?" she asked.

"No, I'm just considering the possibility."

"My father was an honest man, Frank. Yes, he used coke, but look at the incredible stress in his life. You don't know what it's like with all that pressure on you, every minute, night and day, year in and year out. It's a meat grinder, Frank. People need a release."

"Some need it. Most don't. Okay, your father needed it. No, that doesn't make him dishonest. Just a guy who broke the law."

"Like you, Frank. You break the law every time you make a bet. Does that make you dishonest?"

"No." I sighed. "Just a criminal."

Later, on the way home, after dropping off Tina at her apartment, I turned on the all-news radio station to get the Cubs score. They lost, blitzed 8 to 2. The Cubs and I were on a serious losing streak.

29

Even outdoors in the open air I could smell him coming: the odor of clothing fresh from the coin-op cleaner, the sweet pungence of lime after-shave, a whiff of Tullamore Dew, all borne gently on the warm southerly wind blowing softly at my back. Duffy. I felt his strong restraining grip upon my arm as I was about to step into my office building.

"Hello, Frank."

"Duffy. What a pleasant surprise. I hope."

"Let's have coffee."

"Out of your territory, aren't you, Lieutenant?"

"Yeah, yeah." He sighed wearily. "I like to get out in the street once in a while. Gives me the impression I'm still in touch with things."

Side by side we walked slowly down Clark Street toward Hershey's deli near the end of the block. Duffy was overdressed for such a balmy summer day: winter-weight tweed suit and a jaunty cap of woolen houndstooth.

"You're a man with interesting hunches, Wolf," Duffy said. "You ought to play the races."

"You came all the way from downtown to tell me that?"

"You were right about Angler," Duffy said. "Whadda ya think about Osvald? What's the tie-in? You got any hunches?"

"Did they find any prints at the Osvald scene?"

"On what? A cactus?"

Scrawled across the dirty white tile at the base of Hershey's building in spray paint the color of blood was the assertion: LATIN KINGS RULE HERE. Above the crude lettering was

drawn a four-pointed crown and a star of David. Long ago
Hershey gave up his efforts to erase the chronically recur-
ring graffiti. So the statement of territorial domain stays
put, unmolested, except for an occasional dog who takes a
piss on it.

Hershey's deli reeked of garlic, the collective fragrance
of his luscious provender. He waved to me from the cash
register as I came in ahead of Duffy and signaled with fore-
finger that he would be with me in a moment.

Duffy and I took seats opposite each other in a back
booth, Duffy outmaneuvering me to sit facing the entrance.

The waitress came and set glasses of ice water before us.
Duffy ordered pancakes, sausage, orange juice, and coffee. I
ordered a lean pastrami on rye, coffee, and chocolate cheese-
cake.

"Look at me," Duffy ordered, sitting ramrod straight,
chest expanded, chin up, a sliver of a smile on his lips. "Notice anything different?"

I took a close look at his face and neck and saw nothing
unusual. "No more ring around the collar?"

"Come on, Wolf, don't play with me," he said. "Can't you
see the difference?"

"I'm sorry, Lieutenant, I guess I missed it."

"I quit smoking and my blood pressure's way down."

"Good for you, Duffy."

"But don't you notice?"

"Notice what?"

"My nose ain't as red as it used to be."

I looked closely at Duffy's nose, but could detect no difference in its color. "I can't see it. But don't go by me. I'm
getting nearsighted. Shouldn't you give up booze too? That's
also been known to cause a rosy nose."

"One vice at a time, Wolf. I'm still withdrawing from
nicotine. Breaking a habit ain't easy, believe me."

"Don't worry, I believe you."

"This is my second breakfast," Duffy announced. "Since
I stopped smoking I can't stop eating. You think I'll blow up
like a balloon? I'm at that age, you know."

"You'll be all right. Start working out in the police gym."

"Yeah, you're right. I got to get back into shape. Anyway,
look, Wolf, I want to talk to you about the Nockerman murder."

"Really? I thought you'd never bring it up."

"Tell me everything you know."

"I know what you know, Duffy."

"Frank, don't bullshit me. This Nockerman thing started as a simple homicide. Now it's a fucking epidemic with Angler and Osvald part of the package. You got to help me, Frank."

"I don't have clue one, Duffy," I said. "When I first came on the case, who'd I have as suspects? Nocky's girlfriend, his business associate, clients, daughter—"

"Don't forget the Jap," Duffy interrupted.

"The Japanese houseman," I continued, "and the ex-wife, Mrs. Nockerman. But she was the one who hired me, so I ruled her out right away. Then Angler and Osvald get knocked off by the same gun halfway across the country, which probably eliminates all the initial suspects. At least they didn't pull the trigger, although they could have hired someone to do it. But I've talked to all these people and they look clean. Lane might be into something kinky at his office. Maybe a little embezzling from Nockerman. I got nothing sure, just a hunch."

"Wolf, I've already figured that myself. Tell me something I don't know."

"Can we work out a trade?"

"You son-of-a-bitch." Duffy smiled.

The food was brought and set before him. He hunched over his plate and noisily commenced eating.

I sipped my coffee.

"I got something real interesting for you," Duffy said. He poured more syrup on his pancakes, spooned sugar into his coffee. "You tell me first, then I'll tell you."

"You promise?"

"I swear," Duffy solemnly proclaimed.

So I told him almost everything—except that Nockerman's ex-wife had been a brokerage client of her late husband's even after their divorce, and that Angler, Osvald, and Teddy Lane had also been his clients. I also left out some other odds and ends, like the part about the ballbusters who wanted me off the case. I didn't want the Chicago P.D. getting in my way, and I wanted to know more than the cops did.

"You didn't tell me a hell of a lot, Wolf," he said.

"That's all I have. Now it's your turn."

He sopped up pools of syrup with a forkful of pancakes, chewed, swallowed, slurped coffee to sluice it all down.

"The feds are looking into this Nockerman thing," he said.

"Which feds? Justice? Treasury? The F.B.I.?"

"Feds. Period. That's all I can say right now."

"That's not enough. There's all kinds of feds. Who came in on this? The Commodity Futures Trading Commission? Treasury Department people? Customs and Immigration? The Drug Enforcement Agency?"

"The D.E.A? What the hell would they be doin' in on this?"

"I gave you some information, Pat. You didn't give me shit. How'm I ever gonna trust you again?"

"All right, all right." Duffy sighed. "The federal narcs are on the case. I heard about it on the Q.T. from a guy I know in the federal attorney's office."

"Give me some specifics. Who's being investigated? How'd the feds know to come into this in the first place?"

"That's all I know, Frank. I swear."

"Bullshit. You're fishing to see what I got."

He chuckled. "You're a real hard-ass, Wolf. I'm telling you all I know. I can't get nothing more right now. You know those feds, they don't usually cooperate much with the locals. We play ball, but they don't. It's all one way. They want everything for themselves, the glory *and* the gravy. When they're done, we get what's left. Jesus, I'd love to crack this fucking thing before they do. Listen, Wolf, whaddaya got on this dope angle? I mean beyond just Nockerman's using?"

"Nothing, but I'll be looking for something from now on."

We finished eating and Duffy, graciously, as always, permitted me to buy his meal.

I stopped at the cash register on the way out to pay the bill. Duffy stood at my side as Hershey rang it up.

"You fix that device of yours yet?" Hershey asked, counting out change from a twenty.

"What's the device?" Duffy asked. He was nosy by nature, a failing peculiar to cops, P.I.'s, and reporters.

I didn't want to offer lengthy explanations. "Nothing," I said.

"What's the device he's talking about?" Duffy insisted.

"Catalytic converter on my car," I said. "I flunked the emission test."

"You're full of shit," Duffy said. "But thanks for breakfast."

30

During the next few days Tina was lost in a frenzy of last-minute preparations for the gallery opening. I did not see her until late every evening, when we met at her apartment. We'd eat a quiet supper, then retired almost immediately afterward to the sumptuous master bedroom, where I massaged her back as an antidote to her physical and mental fatigue and as a prelude to our lovemaking, which was nonetheless vigorous for all her complaints of exhaustion.

Toward the end of the week I had arranged for two interviews, one with the president of the bank where Osvald, the murdered banker, had been employed as vice president of operations, the other with Osvald's son.

The president of the bank was a Mr. Ecru, a well-tailored eunuchoid gnome of sixty or so with close-cropped salt-and-pepper hair and a face like Gertrude Stein. His eyes were a silvery green, the color of faded currency. He greeted me in a whining tenor, that unctuous, self-aware voice that bankers use to say "No" when you ask to borrow their money. He received me in his paneled office like a feudal lord granting a begrudging audience to one of his vassals.

"Mr. Wolf, how very nice of you to come. Sorry I can't spend more time with you."

Nice of me to come? I had to beg and threaten him for an appointment.

"I hope we can get right to the point, Mr. Wolf," Ecru announced, staring up at me from his desk. Standing at Ecru's right was some corporate factotum; a tall, balding, bespectacled gent; lean, silent, and morose in a midnight-blue suit. He reeked of cologne and Clorets. "This is Mr. Krest," Ecru said, "vice president and chief counsel here at the bank. I'd like him to sit in on this."

"Good idea," I said.

"Let's be comfortable, shall we?" Ecru crooned, rising from his chair. He took me by the arm and led me sound-lessly across the deep pile carpet to a cluster of furniture arrayed on the far side of the room. Krest followed two steps behind us.

Ecru reclined with aristocratic aplomb, legs crossed, on a tufted black leather couch. Krest sat at the other end, yellow legal pad in his lap, pencil at the ready. I sat facing them in one of those straight-backed, hard-seat, barely uphol-stered French provincial chairs deliberately designed to in-flict agonies on your spine.

"Tell me what you know about Mr. Osvald," I said to Ecru.

"First tell me what you know," Ecru said.

"Not a hell of a lot."

"There's only one reason I consented to talk with you, Mr. Wolf," Ecru said, his voice taking on a slight edge. "We agreed to trade information. I want you to tell me what is known about Mr. Osvald, and if there's anything that could reflect badly on the bank or damage its reputation in the financial community."

"Have the cops been here to question you yet?" I asked.

"Yes. And they promised to be back again. I must say, I didn't enjoy dealing with them. I also got a call from the Barstow police. They might fly up here to interview me."

"Did the Chicago cops tell you about Nockerman and Angler?"

"No, they told me nothing. I'm aware, of course, that they were murdered. Both men had accounts here."

"Is that all you know? There's nothing more?"

"That's all I've got at the moment. I might have more later. But right now I'm counting on you to fill me in."

"First tell me about your Mr. Osvald," I said.

"Well," Ecru began, "Ervin Osvald was very much a hands-on executive. He was completely familiar with every bank operation, and made it a point to oversee the whole thing. In fact, there were complaints once in a while from the other V.P.'s that he was making a pest of himself. But his books were impeccable and his operation ran perfectly."

"What about Osvald's personal life?" I asked.

"I'm afraid I can't help you," Ecru answered.

"Let's not bullshit each other, Mr. Ecru," I said. "An important officer of your bank has been murdered. If you think the cops are a pain in the ass, wait till the feds and the bank examiners get here. They'll be all over this place like flies on shit. They'll turn this operation upside down and inside out. Think of all the bum publicity. You'll have a plague of TV reporters poking mikes up your nose asking why a vice president of your bank was murdered. What'll your depositors think? There'll be rumors and whispers, maybe even a run on the bank. The board of directors will want your head on a plate, Mr. Ecru."

Ecru blinked repeatedly as he considered the possibilities. "Yes," he said quietly, "it could become rather unpleasant."

"Look, the sooner I find out why Osvald was murdered, the sooner the bad publicity is all forgotten. Assuming there is no connection between his murder and the bank."

Krest, who had been no more than a silent observer until now, spoke to me then in a voice as sweet and sticky as the glaze they pour over candied yams. "Mr. Wolf, what we want to avoid here at all costs is negative publicity for the bank that could eventuate in a shareholder suit or an unwarranted decline in the market price of our stock."

Ecru nodded his head in affirmation. "Exactly."

"Therefore, we'd be delighted to cooperate with you in your investigation," Krest continued, "providing we have your assurance that any information you develop regarding the bank, its operations, and employees, will be held in strictest confidence. That means, naturally, no leaks to the press."

"Naturally," I said.

Krest smiled and said, "In lieu of a written contract, we'll have to accept your word, Mr. Wolf. I know, however, that you're a man who can be trusted."

"Who told you?" I asked.

"One of our customers," Krest said.

"Was it Tina Nockerman?" I asked.

The slight smile on Krest's face said *yes,* but he uttered a curt, "I can't comment on that."

"All right, tell me what you know about Mr. Osvald."

Ecru sank further into the couch, as if he were being devoured by quicksand. "Osvald was a superior executive. But his personal life took on some unseemly overtones a few years ago after his wife died."

"Unseemly overtones? What the hell are you talking about?"

"I understand he suddenly became interested in young women," Ecru said. "I must confess that I employed a detective agency for a few months to keep Osvald under surveillance to see if there was anything excessive in his spending or irregular in his work. Frankly, I'm terribly embarrassed about the whole thing—I mean my 'spying' on him, so to speak. But as president of this bank, I have obligations and responsibilities. Well, nothing unusual was discovered, and in fact, Osvald became even more conscientious about his work. Except, he wasn't staying late or on weekends anymore. In fact, he started traveling—Europe, the Caribbean, South America, Las Vegas. And always a young woman with him. He was engaged to several of them, and sometimes more than one at a time. Unofficially, of course. He thought that was quite funny. Bragged to me about it incessantly. He seemed to be a very happy man who enjoyed his life thoroughly. And he was spending a lot more than he earned here at the bank."

"Did you ask him where he got the money?"

"Yes. He said he was speculating in the futures market. I told him to stop. I told him he had a highly sensitive position here at the bank, and playing commodities was dangerous. He refused; in fact, he told me to go to hell, in a good-humored way, you understand. We've been associates for years. And of course, I had the highest regard for his abilities as an executive. But I was upset by his rather unorthodox life."

"Unorthodox?"

"For a banker, yes. You know, the glitzy women, sports cars, gambling in Vegas. He even bought a condo in Aspen. That's not your image of the good gray banker."

"Had a good time, didn't he?"

"Maybe too good a time," Ecru said.

"For a banker, anyway," I said. "But tell me, when did all this begin?"

"About seven years ago."

Just about the time, I thought, when everything else began too: Nockerman's sudden upsurge in income, and the incredible killings in the market of certain Nockerman clients—Osvald himself, of course, and Angler, Lane, and Mrs. Nockerman. I didn't think it was coincidence.

"I needn't tell you, Mr. Wolf," Ecru said, "how very upset I am about all this. I'm willing to pay you, that is, the bank is willing to retain your services so that any information you uncover about Mr. Osvald is directed to our attention. That is, to my attention. I know we have your word that you'll keep us informed, but we'd like to give you a little incentive. And of course, only you, I, and Mr. Krest need know about this."

"What incentives?"

Ecru said, "We'd be delighted to talk to you about a personal loan at a quite favorable rate, should you be interested."

"First you want to hire me," I said, "then you want to loan me money. How come I got so lucky with you people?"

"Because I want us to understand one another," Ecru said. Krest stood beside him, nodding his head in agreement, droplets of sweat glittering on his forehead. Then, as if he were speaking for the benefit of the concealed wire he apparently thought I might be wearing, he said loudly and theatrically, "We are in the business of loaning money, you know. At any rate, Mr. Wolf, you will keep everything strictly confidential, and you will keep us informed of all developments, won't you?"

"You can put that in the bank," I said.

Ecru huffed and wheezed as he struggled up from the couch. He offered me his flaccid hand. It was warm and moist and slightly tremulous.

"Good of you to come, Mr. Wolf," he said. "When you have something to report on Osvald, phone me direct at the bank on my unlisted line." He handed me a black and gold business card embossed with his name and private number.

"Thanks. And keep your stocks up."

* * *

I had no intention of doing anything for them. What the hell have banks ever done for me? Bankers and juice men, two of a kind, hustlers working the same territory on opposite sides of the street.

31

Later in the week I met with Ervin Osvald, Jr., in Lincoln Park at high noon. The air was humid and motionless, a dense blue-gray haze that smelled of chlorine and low-octane ethyl. We sat on a bench near the zoo, within earshot of the rookery and the anguished squawking of captive birds. The cops had already talked with Osvald, and I was afraid he might have given them something he'd forget or decline to give me.

Ervin Osvald, Jr., was a tall, gangly man in his late thirties with an oddly protuberant belly. He was horse-faced and toothy, and chopped words as he spoke. With his forehead convoluted in spasms of thought, and his eyelids fluttering nervously beneath a beetle-brow, he reminded me of Richard Nixon.

"I always try to have lunch outdoors," he said. "Being cooped up in an office is so unnatural, isn't it?" As he spoke, he munched on a sandwich of sprouts and whole wheat. "It pains me to say this," said Osvald, "but I'm suing to break Dad's will. He left a substantial amount to his fiancée." He uttered the word fiancée with deliberate irony.

"He did leave you a little something, didn't he?" I asked.

"The bulk of the estate, yes. But some of it went to my father's bimbo."

Osvald suddenly laughed, exposing his long teeth in a lewd smile. He shook his head in amused disapproval. "Dad was quite a cocksman, you know? I admired him greatly."

He finished his main course and produced a see-through

plastic sack of seeds, nuts, and dried fruits. The mixture looked like bird food.

"Will you join me?" he asked, proffering the bag.

"Thanks, I'll pass."

A continuous procession of joggers breezed by us.

"My father and I were very close," Osvald said. "It was money and women that came between us. I handled Dad's finances, including his taxes, up to about eight years ago. Then he started speculating in the futures market, using commodity tax straddles, playing the gold and silver markets. I thought he was getting quite reckless, although I must say he made loads of money. Then his wife died suddenly. Off the record, I was not terribly upset—she was not my mother. Dad divorced my mother about twenty-five years ago to marry this woman, a person I thought loud, crude, and vulgar. But I made it a point to be civil to her. Dad loved her and I loved him. Anyway, about eight years ago, when Dad started making some heavy cash in the markets, his second wife died and he started to party like a wild man. I didn't like it and I said so. I told him he'd destroy his career at the bank, and ruin his health besides. He told me to stuff it, but not that politely. We had a terrible quarrel. I never handled his taxes again. We haven't been close since then."

"Tell me one more thing, Mr. Osvald. Did your father use dope?"

"Yes, unfortunately. Cocaine. It ruined his health and his life. Along with those sleazy broads of his. How'd you know about the drugs?" he asked.

"I guessed. Did you know Mr. Nockerman?"

"Dad's broker? I never met him, but I heard so much about the man, I got sick of it. Dad wasn't the kind to get excited about people, but Mr. Nockerman really impressed him. How Dad admired that man—his lifestyle, his daring, his knowledge of the markets. They made a lot of money together. And when the stock market fell out of bed, Nockerman wasn't hurt at all. Claims he saw it coming months in advance, and had established large short positions in major stocks. I understand everyone took a bath, and Nockerman made a fortune."

"Did your father ever do any special favors for Nockerman?"

"Like what?"

"I don't know, like maybe something above and beyond the call of duty at the bank?"

"You mean something improper? No way. When it came to business, Dad was a straight shooter."

"Take a wild guess—who killed your father?"

"Probably some hopped-up bimbo, disappointed in love."

I hadn't heard the term *hopped-up* in years.

"You think the same bimbo killed Nockerman?" I asked. "They were shot by the same gun, you know."

"You're the private dick, you tell me."

"If I told you what I think, you'd call me nuts," I said.

"Tell me."

"I think your father and Nockerman were doing something illegal together. Like maybe they were in the dope business."

"Pardon me for saying so, Mr. Wolf, but you're nuts."

32

The night of the opening I picked up Tina early. She looked like a perfume ad in *Harper's Bazaar,* sensual, mysterious, and delectable in her billowy silk dress of deep maroon.

As we drove to the gallery she smoked nervously and delivered a rancorous tirade on barbaric art critics who composed their reviews with a meat-ax or the overly erudite who wrote reams of impenetrable gibberish. Then she denounced fickle collectors with more money than taste and an insatiable hunger for novelty, and museum curators who were a mix between fund-raisers and cultural impresarios with an obligation to throw boffo shows à la Phineas T. Barnum.

I had no doubt she believed what she said, but she said it without passion; and so her comments sounded to me like something she had read in a magazine, or had heard from artists or her art dealer colleagues.

She raged for a while, then, apparently exhausted, she sighed and said, "Don't mind me, I'm a little edgy. By the way, I meant to tell you, someone from my bank phoned me and asked about you. I gave you an excellent reference."

"Why'd they call you?"

"They wanted Mother, actually. When you called them for your appointment, you told them she hired you, remember? I told them she was in Europe and I was handling her business while she was gone. They wanted to know about you. Were you a man of character? Could you be trusted? I told them you were—what's the expression?—a stand-up guy. I neglected to tell them we were lovers."

It was almost seven when we arrived at the gallery. The place was empty except for Byron, the artist; Brenda, his beautiful young female friend; and Gerry, Tina's assistant. Introductions were made all around, and I had my hand squeezed just a little too hard by the strapping Byron, a man over six feet tall, dressed in what seemed to me—in my terminal cynicism—as a deliberately ill-fitting brown tweed suit.

Tina left us to make a hasty, final reconnaissance around the gallery, straightening a painting or two, adjusting a bouquet of flowers on the teakwood desk near the entrance, checking to see that the gallery guestbook was open to the proper page. She returned, somewhat breathless, brushing away strands of vagrant hair from her face.

"I'm getting nervous," she said. "The crowds will be coming soon."

"I sincerely hope so," said Byron.

Tina sailed by me, holding the elbows of the men on either side of her, talking excitedly about the art and the artist, first to one, then to the other, her head swiveling back and forth like a spectator at a tennis match. She caught my eye as she passed, flashed me a wink of complicity, but her smile seemed forced, fearful, uncertain.

By the time the last first-nighters had straggled out of the gallery, six paintings had been sold, and four were being considered. The major art critics had come, and were not seen to frown or retch, and that was regarded as a triumph. Furthermore, the artist did not get drunk and insult the wrong people, although Tina said that perhaps a little impropriety now and then on Byron's part might help establish him as a legendary rogue—some people believe that gross misconduct in an artist is the incontestable mark of genius.

Some friends of Tina's threw a little party for the artist and some special guests in their North Side apartment after the opening. As I drove there along Michigan Avenue, alone in the car with Tina, she complained bitterly that so many of her father's friends in the commodity business had not come to her opening.

"Not even Teddy came. I guess now that Daddy's gone

everybody's abandoned me. You know, Frank, Daddy was right. He said everything's a commodity. People, friendship, loyalty."

"Are you sure they knew about it?"

"Frank, I telephoned them personally. And I sent written invitations besides. I tell you, people suck. Unless you can do something for them, nobody knows you're alive."

I said nothing. I know how someone feels when a mood like this comes on. I've been there myself, countless times. You can't say anything, you can't do anything—nothing makes it better, just time, and maybe a bottle of good Scotch.

33

The party was held in one of those nineteenth-century Astor Street town houses, scrupulously restored to its original magnificence. Lofty ceilings, brass doorknobs and window pulls, sumptuous woodwork varnished to a high gloss, the decor and furniture a tossed salad of antique and contemporary.

Tina introduced me to a few people, then with Byron on her arm disappeared into the intimate gathering of some fifty to sixty people.

I meandered about from room to room, admiring the art, the Tiffany lamps, and the good-looking women of every age. For an hour or more, I watched, listened, and drank Scotch. Inevitably, I got bored with art-world gossip—it was just like gossip from any other world.

I looked around for Tina and saw her across the living room chatting with some people. She appeared somewhat tired, her face drawn, her posture not as erect and regal as usual. Abruptly, she walked away from the group and disappeared into the dark corridor off the hallway. She seemed dizzy, almost reeling as she moved; too much champagne, perhaps. And she was probably exhausted from all the work she had done preparing for the opening. I followed her and saw her go into the bathroom.

"Tina, are you all right?"

There was no answer.

The door was unlocked, so I pushed it open. I saw her bent over the sink. In her nostril was a long, cylindrical object that appeared to be a straw; she held it tenderly between thumb and two fingers against a small hand mirror that rested on the marbleized countertop. On the mirror was a thin line of white powder: cocaine.

She glanced at me for an instant without turning her head—no more than a quick movement of her eyes, furtive and ultimately indifferent. Then she looked back to what lay before her on the mirror, lowered her head to see her own image beneath the line of coke, closed her eyes and took a noisy snort.

I winced as I watched her. She lifted her head, removed the straw, smiled strangely, and sniffed in three or four more times.

I looked at her in disbelief. "Why, Tina?"

"I'm nervous and tired from the opening, Frank. You can't imagine what a strain it's been. Want a toot?" she asked.

"No."

"Why not?"

I didn't answer.

"I've got more," she said. "You sure you don't want a taste?"

"You know that stuff will kill you," I said.

"I am not an addict, Frank. I can walk away from it."

"Then quit now."

"Why don't you quit? You think compulsive gambling is different than this?"

"No," I said. "They're just two different ways to self-destruct."

"Then clean up your own act before you start advising me."

"I know what you're going through, Tina. I'll call Weiss Memorial. You'll go into their drug rehab program."

"I don't need it, Frank. I can control this."

"Tomorrow you're going into a drug program. I'll make the arrangements."

"Not yet."

"Right now."

"I'm not ready, Frank." She looked at me, silent.

In one quick step I crossed the space between us and wrapped her in my arms. She felt small, cold, tremulous.

"I want you to stop using," I said.

"Because you love me?"

"Because I want you to stay alive."

"I swear to you, Frank, I'm just a social user. And once in a while, when I'm tired, or feeling down, I—"

I interrupted her. "Then it should be easy for you to quit."

As I drove Tina home she dozed with her head on my shoulder.

"Don't be angry with me, Frank," she murmured.

"I'm not angry at you, baby."

"You'll stay with me tonight?"

"Yeah, I'll stay with you."

"Can we go to your place, Frank?"

"Sure."

"Don't leave me, please. Don't go away."

There was a more willing submissiveness in her love-making that night. Even her flesh seemed softer, more malleable. I made love to her mindlessly, with little sense of the person I held in my arms and who provided me with such intense pleasure.

Later, as we lay in each other's arms, she said in a voice heavy with impending sleep, "Frank . . . I'm not going into a drug program. I'll quit on my own. I promise."

I know all about promising to quit a powerful addiction. I used to promise my ex-wife all the time that I'd quit gambling. And I had alcoholic friends who were always swearing off, then getting loaded again. But maybe Tina wasn't that far gone.

"All right, Tina, try it. But you start using again, I'm going to make you get help."

Tina woke me about six in the morning. She was dressed and on her way out.

"I've got to run, Frank. I've got a million things to do."

"Wait a minute, I'll drive you."

"No, I've got to go home and change. I've already called a cab. It's waiting downstairs."

She leaned down to peck me on the lips and was gone.

"I'll call you later," she said, and walked out the door.

34

I bought all the papers, a *Racing Form,* a large container of black coffee, and went to my office. I owed Freedo six grand plus the vig, and I was afraid he'd be getting antsy soon, maybe start twisting my arm a little to pay him. I phoned Nate Klipstein, a lawyer friend of mine who owed me some money, and left a message on his machine for him to call me. Maybe I could get paid if I squawked loud enough.

I browsed through the *Racing Form* and found an old pal in the feature at Arlington, a horse I knew from last year who made a lot of cash for me. He looked sensational, four consecutive wins at a mile, his last win just two-fifths off the track record at that distance. Nice workouts for six furlongs. Fastest horse in the race, without a doubt. And the season's winningest jockey was up, an aggressive kid with brass balls. The morning line was even money, so there was no sense to bet it place or show. The shot was to put it all on the nose. I telephoned Freedo.

"You owe me six grand plus, Frankie," he told me. His tone was not congenial.

"I want to bet five grand on a horse in the seventh at Arlington."

"Five grand on one fucking horse? You fucking crazy?"

"Goddamn it, Freedo, don't jinx me. Will you book it?"

"Who's the horse?"

I told him.

"To win?"

"Yeah."

"You got the money, Frank?"

"Hey, don't worry, you'll be paid."

"Because if you don't have the money, it's your fucking ass, my dear friend. You lose this, you're in nine grand plus the vig. You gotta come in right away and settle up."

"What's the matter? You can't carry me for a few grand? I was into you for forty-two grand once. Didn't I pay you?"

"Sure you did, Frank. But you took too long. The Man don't like that. We lose, we pay right away, no? Look, Frankie, far as I'm concerned you're good for it. If it were up to me, I'd say what the hell. But it ain't me, Frank. This comes right from the top. The Man says when you're in this deep you gotta settle up before I can take more of your action."

"You're cutting me off after all the money I dropped? What the hell is this, Freedo?"

"Hey, Frankie, in my book you're good people. But I'm just a workin' stiff, same as you. The Man tells me somethin', it's law. Your horse loses, I'll see you tonight. Tomorrow latest. You *capishe*?"

"Yeah, I *capishe*."

I was walking the wing again, way out there near the tip, and the plane kept getting hit by heavy downdrafts. You know the sensation: you're cruising at thirty-five thousand feet and suddenly your seat drops out beneath you. Your bowels clench up like a fist. Slight turbulence, the captain calls it. A fearsome, incomparable kick, like the shoot-the-chute; I hate it, I love it.

I read the morning papers to becalm myself. There was a story about a total eclipse of the moon coming next Tuesday. I made a note about it in my desk calendar.

Tina called me about ten from her gallery.

"I'm sorry I had to run off this morning. I miss you. Take me to dinner tonight?"

"Sure," I said. "And write this down in your appointment book so you won't forget. Next Tuesday there's a total eclipse of the moon. We'll watch it together from my roof. I'll make us a little something to eat. We'll dine outside at Wolf's Roof Garden. Very exclusive joint."

"It's a deal. I'll bring the wine."

* * *

I spent the rest of the day on the phone, chasing leads in the Nockerman case, talking to former clients of his, business associates, acquaintances. Nothing.

At ten after five I called Freedo. He gave it to me in a soothing, consoling voice, as if telling me someone had died.

"I'm sorry, Frank. Your horse lost. Ran out of the money. You owe me twelve thousand, one, total, which includes all the vig. You got to pay us the whole thing now, Frank, like you promised. I expect to see you here tonight. Or first thing in the morning. *Ciao,* Frankie."

I was stunned. That feeling of being dipped in Vicks spread over me. I broke into a cold, mentholated sweat.

The phone rang. It was Klipstein.

"I just got your message, Frank. I've been in court all day."

"I need that money you owe me," I said.

"No way. I'm tapped right now."

"I got to have it, Nate. I owe my bookmaker twelve grand."

"You're a degenerate gambler, Frank. You need help."

"I need what you owe me."

"Soon as I can. Maybe three, four weeks. Listen, Frank, what about doing some work for me? I'd have to owe you the money until the case is settled, but—"

"You're worthless, Nate," I told him, and hung up the phone.

35

I owed heavy cash again, and I felt that all-too-familiar tornado in the gut, along with the usual horrifying euphoria. So long, symmetry.

I had about three hundred in cash, so I'd have to scare up another eleven grand, eight. Impossible. I had no liquid assets—no savings accounts, no stocks, bonds, insurance policies, nothing. I could pawn my TV, radio, stereo, tape recorder, camera, typewriter, and my other hockable high-tech gadgets, but why should I deprive myself of those necessities and pleasures? Besides, together they wouldn't amount to two grand; I know, I've had them all in hock before. And I couldn't sell my car, of course. I had no choice but to tell Freedo the bad news: I didn't have his money and I'd have to cop an easy payment plan.

That evening Tina and I ate at a seafood joint on LaSalle Street, north of the river. Halfway through my lobster I said, "I lost a lot of money today."

She stopped eating, lifted her head. "Gambling?"

I nodded. "I owe a guy twelve grand and I don't have it."

Without hesitation she said, "I'll loan it to you. Tomorrow, first thing when the bank opens I'll get you the cash. Pay me back whenever you can."

"That would certainly make things easier for me. For the time being. But sooner or later I'd get in the same jam again. I know myself. It would go on forever. I'd just keep taking your money, playing and losing. Eventually, I'd tap you out. Or you'd get sick of me."

"You've got to get help, Frank."

"Yeah, I know. But don't tell me go to Gamblers Anonymous. That's for losers. I'll straighten out on my own. I hope. Because I wouldn't want you to be involved with me if I'm still gambling this way."

"Okay, Frank, you're an intelligent, reasonable man. You'll beat this thing. Meanwhile, you need money. I'll give it to you."

"A few years ago I would've taken your money. I'd be embarrassed and humiliated. But I wouldn't care. I'd do anything to stay in the action. But I'm through with all that. I don't want it to destroy what we have together. Like it did with someone else I once cared for."

"Take the money, Frank, and pay these people. Please. I don't want you to get hurt."

"I won't be hurt. I'll work something out. I've done it before."

"You sure?"

"Yes."

"All right, Frank, but if you need the money, you got it."

"Thanks," I said. "I hope your self-discipline's better than mine."

"I haven't had anything since Byron's party."

"Good. Stay clean."

"You too."

"I'm going to try."

36

About noon the next day I drove out to Freedo's with three hundred in my pocket. His place was empty except for the handful of guys in the back taking bets over the phone.

"Here," I said, handing him a wad of bills. "I owe you the rest."

"You're short? What the fuck is this?"

"I'll pay you five hundred a month."

"You fuckin' lied to me, Frank. You told me you had the money. You realize you're in deep shit here?"

"I'm going to pay you every cent, Freedo."

"You fuckin' right you are. I warned you last time this happened, Frank. You better raise that cash. Steal it, rob a bank, put your mother on the street. I don't give a fuck. Just get it."

"Talk to your people. Tell 'em I'm sincere. See what you can do for me."

"This is my ass, too, Frank. I okayed the bet."

"Will you talk to your people?"

"Yeah, yeah, I'll talk. What the fuck else can I do?"

"Tell 'em I'm good for it. I paid 'em off before a couple times. They'll remember me."

"You asshole. What if the Man says you gotta be taught a lesson?"

"Then I'm fucked."

Freedo laughed without smiling. "You're nuts, you know that, Frankie? You're fuckin' crazy."

"Not anymore," I said.

Strange how memory works. Seeing Freedo again reminded me of something he had told me last time I saw him, just after Nockerman was killed: *"Nocky hung out with some funny people."*

"Freedo, remember you told me you saw Nockerman around town with some funny people?"

"Yeah, sure, I remember."

"Who were you talking about?"

"I should tell you? After what you pulled on me?"

"I could make some money on it if I knew. Help me pay off what I owe here."

"What? There's a reward out or something?"

"No, just business."

"Okay, but you got to forget it came from me."

I nodded. "Absolutely."

"I used to see him all the time with a guy named Joey Watt. Strictly a low-class type, strong-arm shit, muscle business. That kinda thing. Although I heard a few years ago he started putting holes in people for money. But bush league only, free-lance. Smart people don't want nothin' to do with him."

"What's he look like?"

"Snappy dresser, but a face like some woodpeckers had a picnic on it."

It sounded like he was describing the guy who visited Mrs. Angler.

"You saw him around town with Nockerman?"

"Yeah, but mainly at the racetrack. He goes almost every day during the season. He's a freak for horses."

The Outfit must hold Watt in extremely low regard—in fact, they might be downright hostile to him, otherwise Freedo wouldn't have told me so much.

"He have a rap sheet?"

"You kidding? Long as my schmuck."

"Thanks, Freedo."

"Hey, hey," he raised both hands in a gesture that said *back off.* "Don't tell me 'thank you.' I didn't do nothin' for you, Frank. Your dick's in the wringer on this twelve grand. I hope the Man's in a generous mood when I talk to him about you."

"Me too."

37

I couldn't find Watt's telephone number in the Chicago book or any of the suburban directories. I called information and was told he had an unpublished number. So I phoned my friend at Illinois Bell and got what I wanted, plus Watt's current address. He was living in a residential hotel just south of the Loop off Michigan Avenue. He had a direct phone line to his apartment, but I called the hotel desk to get his room number.

Later that evening I parked in a tow-away zone across the street from and kitty-corner to Watt's hotel. I was wearing one of my simple disguises, so that neither Watt nor anyone else could make me: gray wig, crew-cut style, and a bushy gray mustache. I put down the sun visor on my car with the sign that said: Cook County Sheriff's Department. Official Business. It was the real thing. I bought it a few years ago from a deputy who needed some quick cash. It would keep the beat cop from giving me a ticket, and prevent my car from getting towed to the pound if I had to leave it parked illegally for a while.

I had my Nikon with motor drive and 300mm telephoto lens. The outfit was strapped around my neck, fully loaded and ready to shoot. I wanted to get a picture of Watt and show it to Mrs. Angler. I thought Watt was the same guy who had come to her house that night looking for her husband and beat her up when he couldn't find him. Same guy who probably found him later and put the hole in his head.

I had a clear view of the hotel entrance and could see anyone who came in or out. I settled down then to the tedium of the stakeout, aeons of boredom that inevitably end with a stiff neck, leg cramps, and a bursting bladder. As always, I had brought along my portable pisser, a wide-mouth, one quart mason jar, in case I was detained more than expected.

About two hours later, shortly before eight o'clock, a guy I assumed to be Watt came out and hailed a cab. There was another guy with him and they were talking to each other, their heads together. I started shooting the man I took for Watt with my camera, the motor drive firing away four frames per second. Unavoidably, the man with Watt was in several shots. Watt looked like a page from GQ, pale blue seersucker suit, pink shirt with long pointed collar and light gray tie, and a white carnation in the buttonhole of his lapel.

But his face was a calamity in flesh, pitted and pock-marked like those ancient crumbling temple ruins deep in the Cambodian jungle. Watt's companion was fortyish, tall, dark, Greek or Italian maybe, remnants of his former muscularity dissolving into fat. He was balding, with salt-and-pepper hair that was teased, blow-dried, and sprayed to give the impression he had more of it. He wore an expensive summer suit of navy blue and a deep-burgundy tie. A taxi pulled up and they both got in, after Watt opened the door in what seemed to me an act of subservience. Then the cab sped off.

I got out of my car and went down to the corner drugstore to telephone Watt's room direct and see if he was there. His answering machine said: "I'm not home. I'll be back later. Please leave your message when you hear the beep."

I crossed the street and went into the hotel, striding purposefully through the lobby as if I belonged there. The desk clerk looked up at me for a moment from his *Enquirer,* blinked once or twice, then returned to his reading.

I went up in the elevator, got off at eight, and found Watt's door at the end of the empty corridor. I had no trouble getting into his apartment—a moment or two of adroit picking and I sprung the lock. Apparently, the man was not too security conscious, another victim of the "it can't happen to me" syndrome, common even to hoods, it seems.

I went in and quietly shut the door behind me. The suite was a barely furnished two rooms, with a tiny kitchen and bath. Not too posh, not too shabby, merely habitable. Just right for the man who doesn't stay home much.

* * *

I was feeling the kick that comes with breaking and entering, the rush from being where you don't belong. I've been told that's why some people stay in the business bust after bust, just for the charge.

I browsed through Watt's living room and kitchen, opened drawers, shoved my hand between the cushions on the couch, looked under the sink, into the cabinets and refrigerator. Nothing worthwhile. I went into the bathroom and checked the medicine cabinet. It was full of the usual patent remedies, including a small box of Dramamine with four tablets missing. According to the expiration date, it was purchased recently.

I went next to the bedroom. There was a king-size bed and a large double closet full of Watt's fancy suits and jackets. I felt around in the dresser drawers, very carefully so as not to upset the neatly stacked layers of socks, shirts, and shorts. I wanted to leave no evidence of my presence. I probed under the mattress, looked beneath the bed, poked around the top shelf of the closet. I searched through his clothing like a pickpocket, hoping to find a matchbook from an Albuquerque motel, an American Express bill for a meal in Barstow, or maybe an airline boarding pass—something to place him at the scene of the Angler or Osvald murders. There was nothing. The place was clean, as if a team of maids had picked up everything and threw it all out.

And I found no guns stashed away, nor did I expect to. No savvy professional would leave a hot piece laying around.

Next to the bed on the nightstand was the phone and an answering machine. I pressed the playback button. There were no messages, only the click when I had hung up.

Then I opened the nightstand drawer and saw something fascinating: four very expensive watches, two gold, one silver, one platinum. They were all ticking away in perfect time—I checked them against my Omega, which was always right on the money. But one of Watt's watches was set exactly an hour earlier, as if he had worn it in a mountain time zone—Albuquerque, maybe?—and forgot to set it back when he returned to Chicago. I was guessing, of course. The watch might have meant nothing; it was far too circumstantial to offer as evidence of anything. But the watch and the Dramamine together added up to an unequivocal *maybe*—Watt *might* have taken a recent trip out West. Hardly enough to tie him to the Angler murder. But if Mrs. Angler could identify Watt from my photograph, and if Tina recognized the man in the photo and remembered seeing him with her father, then I might start making some progress.

I wanted to give the place a more thorough shakedown, but I didn't want Watt to know someone had been there. So I left quietly, walked swiftly down the corridor, slipped out the exit, and took the fire escape to the alley.

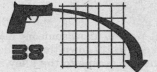

38

I went straight to a custom photo lab on West Superior Street to have the film developed that I shot outside Watt's hotel. There were a dozen good black-and-white pics of Watt, some of which included the second man. I selected the three best of Watt alone, another three which showed him with his associate, and had eight-by-ten prints made. An hour later I was in Mrs. Angler's living room, the photos spread before her on the coffee table.

I pointed to Watt in one of the pictures.

"Is this the man who came to your house looking for your husband, the man who beat you up?"

She looked, then shuddered, closing her eyes tightly.

"That's him."

"You sure?"

"No way I'm gonna forget a creep like that."

"Who's the other guy?"

She studied the prints. "I don't know. What are you going to do now?"

"Throw a net over our good-looking friend here."

"I'd love for you to hurt him real bad."

39

I took root again outside Watt's hotel in the tow-away zone across the street. When he turned up I'd lock a tail on him.

I had shown my photo of Watt to Tina and she had a hazy recollection of having seen him a few times with her father, but beyond that she knew nothing about him. Lane had looked at the shot and said he never saw the man before. Not much help. All I had was Mrs. Angler's positive identification, and my own guess that Watt had been to Albuquerque and killed Angler. And so I sat in my car and waited.

He must have been shacked up somewhere for the weekend, because he didn't show during the sixteen hours I spent watching his hotel Saturday and Sunday. Nor did he return my phone call—I had left a message for him on his answering machine, and gave him the number of a special line I had at my office, a number listed to someone else, and at a different address. This odd arrangement was devised for me by my pal from Illinois Bell in lieu of payment of a marker he owed me from a poker game. I use the line when I don't want people to know there's a P.I.'s office on my end of the phone.

Monday is a work day even in the criminal underworld, although your average thug likes to get a late start, so I expected Watt to turn up by noon, maybe to shave, shower, change clothes. But he never showed, so I went home, slept for six hours, ate breakfast and started again. Still no Watt.

Tuesday night was cool, clear, and very windy, perfect weather for observing the eclipse. It was early summer and the long twilight at last had given way to darkness. The moon cruised fat and brilliant in the sky.

I had spread a blanket out on the roof and laid down a big air mattress. Here we sat and ate the chopped sirloin burgers that I cooked on the grill I lugged there from my apartment.

My portable stereo tape machine was playing softly, a collection of great classic ballads sung by Sinatra. Tina and I danced together slowly to the music. It was pleasant holding her in my arms and looking at her face in the moonlight.

"Remember how the sky used to be filled with stars?" I asked. "Can't see anything now. Too much air and light pollution. In New Mexico the stars are incredible. On a clear winter night the whole sky's lit up. You ever been to the Southwest?"

"No."

"I lived out there for a few years. A long time ago. God, it's great country. Vast, empty, and clean. Like the world must've been in the beginning, before people came along and dirtied it up. I'd like to go back there to live someday."

I looked at my Omega. "The eclipse'll start in about five minutes. Let's stretch out on the blanket and watch."

We sat down and I poured us each a glass of wine.

We looked up into the sky. The shadow of the earth started inching across the lunar face. The night began to darken.

Imagine the horror of the ancients when they witnessed the moon being eaten by some demon. What gods had they failed to propitiate? What ritual had they neglected to perform?

"Here's to the moon," I said. "And all the lovers it ever shined on."

Tina and I touched glasses, and then as I raised my glass to drink, it exploded in my hand.

Blood-red burgundy splattered across my white shirt. An instant later a nearby skylight shattered, as if hit by a sledgehammer. Then a small round hole opened in the mattress and all the air hissed out. Everything happened in two or three seconds, simultaneous with the sharp *crack, crack, crack* of rifle fire.

I leaped on Tina and threw her down flat against the deflated air mattress, covering her with my body. She groaned explosively when I hit her, a sound like the ball carrier makes when he's stopped by a defensive tackle.

We were both panting. There were abrasions on Tina's cheek where she had struck the roof. I could smell the tar of the graveled shingles.

Someone had shot at me with a high-powered rifle. But the gusty wind had blown the shots off target. The shooter had not readjusted his sights for windage. The next cluster would be closer.

"I'm gonna run," I told Tina. "When I get up and start drawing fire, take off in the opposite direction. They want me, babe, not you."

I didn't wait for her reply.

I jumped up and dashed toward the north edge of the roof.

I saw Tina from the corner of my eye. She flew like a wild woman to the other side, never looking behind her.

There were three more shots, two thumped into the roof right behind me, the third hit immediately in front of me.

I saw the brick chimney looming toward me as I ran. I made a headlong dive and rolled behind it.

I saw Tina yank open the access door to the roof and disappear.

I lay flat and motionless, out of breath, feeling the overload on my heart, expecting the shot any second.

Nobody fired at me. At last I felt reasonably certain the sniper had fled, scared away by the noise he had made. I raised my head slowly, cautiously, ready to duck. Nothing. I jumped up and ran across the roof, my footing uncertain against the loose gravel.

A moment later I was back in my apartment. Tina flung her arms around me as I walked in.

"Thank God you're alive," she said. "Are you all right?"

"I seem to be. What about you?" I asked.

"I look worse than I feel."

"Come on, I'll tend to your wounds," I told her.

She was trembling as I led her into the bathroom. I felt the pulse at her wrist. It was beating in double-time.

"You want a drink, babe? It'll calm you down."

She shook her head.

I had her sit on the edge of the tub and I cleaned the abrasions on her face with cotton swabs dipped in alcohol.

"You'll be okay, Tina. No scars."

"What was that all about, Frank? Tell me?"

"I'm not sure," I said. "Did you call the police?"

"No. I didn't even think about it."

"It's too late anyway," I said. "Whoever shot at me's gone by now. I'll go to the cops tomorrow. Meanwhile, it's definitely not safe for you to be with me until I clear this up."

"What is it, Frank? What's it all about?"

"I don't know. Obviously, someone wants me dead." I figured it was Watt. He found out I broke into his apartment, and now he wants to waste me. Although how the hell did he know I'd be on the roof tonight?

"Does it have something to do with Daddy's murder?"

"Possibly," I said. "Think back, Tina, who'd you tell we were going to be on the roof tonight?"

"Nobody . . . I mean I don't remember. My mother, a couple of people at the gallery. A friend or two. Maybe someone at the bank. I really can't recall."

"Why'd you tell your mother?"

"She calls from Europe once a week. Wants to know what I'm doing, who I'm seeing. You know, she's a typical mother."

"You tell anyone else?"

"I don't think so. But what about you? Who'd you tell?"

"Not a soul. Maybe someone's got a bug on my phone."

"Come home with me, Frank."

"No, I'll stay here. Alone. It'll be safer for both of us."

"Please, Frank," she begged. "I need you with me."

"What if someone's following me?"

"They won't get into the Hancock. Security's too good."

"Yeah? Look what happened to your father."

"Please, Frank, I want you at my place tonight."

"Okay. But starting tomorrow I'm not going to be seeing you for a while. Not until I break this thing. Whoever shot at me tonight is going to try it again and he doesn't care if you get in the way."

"Hold me, Frank, I'm frightened."

So was I. I took her in my arms.

40

Neither of us slept well that night. For hours, Tina wrestled with her bedclothes, dozing, waking, talking to me for a few moments before drifting off, then crying out in her sleep and waking to begin the cycle all over again. I held her and for a while she curled up in my arms like a child. But then she would suddenly break from my embrace as if escaping from something and resume her fitful tossing. I didn't sleep much better.

At dawn I was up and dressed and in the kitchen making coffee. From the eighty-ninth floor in the smoky, hazy blue-gray light the city looked out of focus. At this height, and from behind these sealed windows, you can't hear it, smell it, or touch it.

As I poured water into the Mr. Coffee machine I noticed a stack of mail on the kitchen counter. Some impulse, not entirely benign, made me look through it. On several of the envelopes addressed to Tina was Mrs. Nockerman's handwriting. But the return address was a Mrs. R. Stone in Palm Springs, California. I had no doubt about the handwriting—it was Mrs. Nockerman's. I remembered the first retainer check she had given me with that peculiar scrawl of hers, a combination of upper- and lowercase letters, as if the writer were schizoid.

I took a letter out of its envelope and read the salutation:

Dear Tina,

I skipped past the text to see how it was signed:

Love, Mom

Obviously Mrs. Nockerman was hiding out in Palm Springs under a phony name, while everyone thought she was touring Europe.

A moment later Tina came in, drowsy-faced and barefoot, beautiful in her pink nightgown, long hair uncombed.

"Good morning." She smiled.

"Good morning," I said. "What's your mother doing in Palm Springs?"

She looked at me wide-eyed, puzzled.

"You read my mail?"

"Not exactly. Just your name, your mother's name, and the return address."

For an instant her mind seemed to be racing. Then she sat down slowly at the kitchen table.

"Mama is terribly afraid," she said dreamily.

I stood over her, leaning on the table with both hands, bending to look into her eyes.

"Why'd you lie to me, Tina?"

"Mama made me swear not to tell you. Or anyone."

I sat down opposite her. "You're going to have to tell me."

"I can't." She looked frightened.

"You'd make a great pair of criminals. The letters come right here to your apartment, in your mother's handwriting. What if someone intercepts your mail?"

"I never thought of that."

I asked her again, with a calculated edge in my voice, "Why's your mother hiding?"

The tears dropped silently as she spoke. "A few years ago, after Mom and Dad got divorced, they went into some kind of a partnership together. Don't ask me what it was, because I don't know. After Daddy was killed, Mom got scared because she thought his murder had something to do with their business. She was afraid that whoever killed Daddy wanted to kill her too. So she told everyone she was going to Europe and went to Palm Springs, instead. She was hoping you'd find the killer before the killer found her."

"Why didn't she tell the police?"

"Because the business was not legitimate."

"What was it?"

"I told you, Frank, I don't know."

"You have no idea? You couldn't even guess?"

"No."

"How'd you know it was illegal?"

"I overheard something. A year or so after the divorce, Daddy had come over for dinner one night. At some point I left the table, but on my way back I heard Daddy tell Mom to be very careful because if she got caught, they might both do some time."

"Caught doing what?"

"I don't know. I just heard a piece of their conversation. I asked Mom about it later, and she admitted that she and Daddy were involved in something, well, maybe questionable. But she wouldn't go into detail."

"And you left it at that?"

"Yes."

"You were never curious enough to ask more questions?"

"I was curious, but I never asked."

"Why'd your mother hire me?"

"Because she knew you had worked for Daddy. She thought she could trust you."

"Trust me to do what?"

"Find out who murdered Daddy, get the stolen money back, and keep the police and the press in the dark so that she wouldn't get involved."

"This doesn't make a hell of a lot of sense, Tina. Your parents were partners in a crooked business. Someone kills your father and steals a bundle of his money. Your mother thinks the murder is related to their business, and maybe she's next. So she hires me to do what the cops should do. She thinks I'll find the guy who killed her husband, turn him over to the police, and fix things so that she isn't dragged into it? Well, she certainly overestimates my abilities. How in hell does she figure to stay out of all this?"

"Mother was terrified. So was I. We didn't know what to do. I begged her to tell me what Daddy had done to get murdered. She swore she didn't know. She lived in constant fear. Do you know what that's like? Maybe you do after last night. I certainly do. Anyway, Mother was terrified. So she ran. To Palm Springs. She rented a house under an assumed name and planned to stay there until it was all over."

"Why didn't you tell me?"

"Frank, she made me take an oath. She's my mother."

"Okay, babe, I know. You've been through hell."

She nodded, wiped away a tear.

"But don't ever lie to me again," I said.

"I won't. I love you, Frank."

I said nothing.

"You never told me you love me," she said. "Why not, Frank?"

"Because I'm not sure I do. If and when I say it, I'll mean it. And I'll want everything that goes with it."

"You got it."

"I'm going to Palm Springs to talk to your mother," I said.

"I'm coming with you, Frank."

"No, I'm going alone. It's not safe for us to travel together."

"We'll take separate planes."

"No, we won't. I'll go and you'll stay here. In fact, we better not see one another until I wrap this up."

"No, we're going through this together."

"Maybe. But I'm going to Palm Springs alone."

"Please, Frank, be careful. I couldn't bear it if something happened to you too."

Shortly after nine that morning I went to see Duffy and told him about the sniper.

"What the hell you doing, someone's shooting at you?"

I told him about the two guys who tried to scare me off the Nockerman case and gave him a description of both.

"You bring in anybody like that, let me know," I said. "I'll take a look at them."

"Why didn't you come to me right away? You're a pain in the ass, you know, Wolf?"

I nodded.

"Those two guys, who'd you think they were working for?"

"If I knew, I'd have this wrapped up," I said.

"Want to look at some mug shots?"

"Spend a whole year browsing through Who's Who in Crime? Forget it."

"What about last night? Is there a Nockerman connection?"

"Probably." I didn't tell Duffy what I knew about Watt.

"You know where the shots came from?"

"I'm not sure. Send some of your people over to look at my roof and then canvass the surrounding buildings."

"Thanks, Mr. P.I., I didn't quite know how to handle this."

"You're welcome," I said. "And don't bother to ask me if I want police protection. I don't."

"I didn't think so. But watch yourself. And stay in touch, goddamnit. I want to be kept up on this Nockerman business and everything else you're doing."

"Yeah, I'll send you hourly bulletins."

"Should I put a tail on you for a couple days, sort of watch your back for you?"

"No, we'd just step on each other's dicks. But thanks anyway."

47

In the airport before I boarded my plane for Palm Springs, I bought two million bucks worth of insurance, one mil each for my son and daughter. I never did provide for them very well in life, but if my plane crashed, at least they'd have something.

When I stepped off the plane in Palm Springs, the desert air hit me like a blast furnace. I squinted into the sunlight, waiting for my eyes to adjust.

I took a cab to Mrs. Nockerman's place in the foothills of Mount San Jacinto on the west side of town. It was near noon, the desert heat was raging and the streets were empty.

As the cab pulled away, I stood with my small overnight bag before an iron fence enclosing a small compound that included a rambling, multilevel ranch house, garage, and about a half acre of grounds landscaped in the minimal maintenance desert style, i.e., gravel where the grass should be, spiny cactus where the bushes should be, with an occasional palm tree thrust into a patch of earth encircled by terra-cotta brick.

I pressed a button on the gate announcing my presence and gazed into the TV monitor perched high on the fence post. A hot breeze blew in from the other side of the house and I smelled the swimming pool. At last the gate clicked open. A maid in starched whites appeared and escorted me to Mrs. Nockerman.

She lay at poolside on a beach chair, indolent as a lizard on a rock, virtually naked, covered only by a few thin straps and strands of fabric. Her body was still better than good, but there were small ripples of cellulite starting here and there, and her deeply tanned flesh puckered where the Palm Springs sun had scorched it. I looked at her face, and now that I knew she wasn't Tina's natural mother, there seemed to be little resemblance between them. Only the speech patterns were similar, and the broad, brilliant smile, which Mrs. Nockerman used deliberately for effect, and which came to Tina spontaneously.

"I'll tell you up front," she said. "I'm not terribly delighted to see you."

"May I sit?" I asked.

"Go ahead," she said, not too graciously.

I pulled up another beach chair and sat down opposite her. The heat was searing. I felt like a side of beef in a microwave oven. At the far end of the pool, lounging supine on a chaise, was a long slab of suntanned, muscular flesh. A friend of Mrs. Nockerman's, I assumed. He pretended not to take notice of our conversation, but I saw that he was straining to hear.

"Why'd you lie to me, Mrs. Nockerman?"

She studied me for a moment, figuring how to react. Then she smiled, and made her eyes go wide with innocence.

"Lie to you, Mr. Wolf? About what?"

"You told people you were going to Europe, but you came here instead."

"All right," she said, sighing, apparently deciding not to play games. "I was afraid whoever killed Abel might kill me too."

"Who?"

"I don't know."

"Then why'd you think you were in danger?"

"Look, Mr. Wolf, have you made any progress on the case?"

"Not as much as I could've."

"Meaning?"

"You didn't help much, Mrs. Nockerman."

"Really? I think I've been very cooperative. What more could you want from me?"

"For openers, wouldn't we be more comfortable inside?"

"Undoubtedly. But I want to burn off last night's excess, so I'm afraid you'll have to bear with me."

"Then I hope you won't mind." I pulled off my tie, rolled up my sleeves and unbuttoned my shirt to the sternum.

"Take it all off and have a swim," she said. "I won't mind."

"Yeah, maybe later. Now, explain to me why you didn't tell the cops you were afraid of getting murdered."

"I didn't want to get involved."

"In what?"

"Nothing."

"Nothing?"

I noticed the guy stretched out in the beach chair at the far end of the pool was pretending so hard not to listen that he was getting a hernia. I glanced his way, locked onto his eyes and shot him a look that said: I'm wise to you.

I turned back to Mrs. Nockerman. "What business were you in with your husband?"

"Business? Abel and I? I haven't the slightest idea what you mean."

"I know all about it," I said. "Tina told me. She overheard you and your late husband talking about it one night."

"I don't know what you're referring to. All I did was deliver some packages for Abel. New York, L.A., Las Vegas, other places. I don't remember them all."

"What was in the packages?"

She shook her head. "I don't know."

"You were a mule, Mrs. Nockerman. There was dope in those packages you delivered."

"Dope?" Her eyebrows lifted.

"Yes. Cocaine."

"All right, yes," she said, quietly. "I delivered coke for Abel. But I swear to you, I was unaware of it until I found out by accident much later."

"I think you knew all along. Now, who are W. Mayne Angler and Ervin Osvald?"

"Never heard of them."

"They're dead, murdered, part of the same package that includes your late husband."

"Look, Wolf, that's why I ran. When Abel got killed, I figured he was in some dope deal that went sour. Or maybe he screwed somebody in the business. You read about these things all the time. I thought maybe they wanted to kill me, too, since I made the deliveries. That's why I ran. And that's why I lied to you and the police. I thought you'd find out who killed Abel before the cops did, and maybe I could stay out of it."

"Did you know any of your husband's dope-business associates or customers?"

"No, I swear. I just flew to some city, like Dallas for example, left the package in an airport locker, mailed the key to a post office box—Abel always gave me a preaddressed envelope with postage on it. Then I'd take the next plane."

"Why'd you do it?"

"Living well gets to be a habit. I needed the money."

"But you made a fortune in the market during that period."

"What's a fortune? I lead an expensive life. A person can always use a little extra. The truth of it is, Abel forced me to do it. He was handling a managed commodity account for me and making loads of money. But one day he told me that it would stop unless I helped him in this business venture. And of course, he offered to pay me very well besides. I had no idea at the time it was dope. I'll take an oath on that. I'll take a lie detector. I swear on Tina's life, it's true."

"You made Tina part of your deception, Mrs. Nockerman. She lied to me, and she lied to the police. Now you're both in a lot of trouble. Tina I might be able to help. You, I don't know. I may not be able to do anything."

"Please, Wolf, don't tell anyone where I am. These people are crazy. They'll kill me. Did they kill Lane yet?"

"Lane? Why would they want to kill him?"

"He knows everything. He was in it with Abel."

"In the dope business?"

"Yes."

"How do you know that?"

"I know, believe me. You mean he's not dead and he hasn't been arrested?"

"No to both questions."

"He's still in Chicago? He's not hiding out somewhere?"

"No."

"I think I understand something now," she said.

"If you thought Lane had something to do with this, why didn't you tell the police?"

"Lane was their prime suspect. I thought if they didn't have anything on him, then maybe he didn't kill Abel."

"No, maybe not. But if he was in the coke business with Abel, why didn't you tell that to the cops?"

"Because, you dumb bastard, that would have involved me."

"So you ran away from it all and hoped it would eventually blow over?"

"My advice to you, Mr. Wolf, is to get back to Chicago and talk to Teddy Lane. He's the man with all the answers. Meanwhile, I hope you're not going to tell the cops where I am."

"Not unless they ask me."

"If I were you I'd say nothing until this is all over and resolved to my satisfaction. I could make life very easy for you, Mr. Wolf. I know you're having an affair with my daughter, and while you're not my idea of the perfect son-in-law, I've got enough money to help you get started in a real business, not this sleazy private-investigator crap."

"Is that a bribe?" I asked.

"Frankly, yes."

"To do what?"

"Just keep me out of it," she said.

"How?"

"You're a man of the world. Figure out something."

"Do you know your daughter uses cocaine?"

"Yes, I know. I thought she might have given it up by now. I guess bad habits are hard to break. She always was a troublesome child—look at her parents, both alcoholics, both suicides, although the mother drank herself to death."

"You're also a user?"

"Yes, I'm afraid so. That bastard Abel got me started. That's what he had on me. That's why I went to work for him and did what I did. For the coke. You can't possibly know what it's like to be an addict."

"I can guess," I said. "But what puzzles me is your husband. He had loads of money. Why the hell did he get involved with dope?"

"Believe me, he didn't do it for the money. It was a game, a little boy playing cops and robbers, a man-sized thrill for a kid who never grew up. And a way to test his luck and his skill, and to see if he was better than the competition."

"I can understand that," I said. "I'm a gambler myself."

"Look," she said, "I want your promise to keep me out of this. I'll pay you whatever you want. A hundred grand."

A hundred grand? Nice. I could pay off Freedo, take a long vacation with Tina on some Caribbean island, swim, lay in the sun, play a little blackjack in the casino.

"I'm not interested," I said.

"One hundred thousand dollars. Cash." She said it slowly, so I'd savor every syllable, visualize it in neat, banded packages of crisp hundred dollar bills fresh from the bank.

"Sorry, no sale."

"You want more? How much?"

"I'm not selling it," I said.

"Tell me," she insisted, "what'll it take?"

"This isn't the commodity market, Mrs. Nockerman." I had a profound sense of satisfaction telling this millionaire doper she couldn't buy me like a bushel of wheat.

She cocked her head to the side, frowned at me for a moment with blinking eyes in profound disbelief and frustration. Then she told me, "You self-righteous jerk. You're terminated."

"Fired?"

"Yes. For incompetence, malpractice, and dishonesty. Gouging me on your expenses. Doing nothing. Getting nowhere. Threatening people with violence. Breaking the law. Tell the cops whatever you want now. Who in hell's gonna believe a down-at-the-heels, third-rate P.I. like you, trying to get even with a client who canned him?"

"That's not too smart, is it, Mrs. Nockerman?"

"Get out." It was a calm, imperious order, uttered by a woman accustomed to power supported by money.

"You can't fire me. I'll work for nothing."

She turned and signaled to her meatball. He stood up and ambled over, inflating his chest and flexing his lats so I'd know he was a ballbuster. I took a good look at him, but he wasn't one of the beef jerkys who stomped on me a few weeks ago.

"Gene," Mrs. Nockerman said sweetly to her hunk, "this

pain in the ass used to be an employee of mine. I just pulled his plug."

"Have a nice day, mister," Gene said. "But not here."

"Where, then?"

"Just say bye-bye, Wolf."

"Can I ask you a couple questions first?"

He swung, I ducked, then I came up under him and threw a body block with my shoulder to his gut that sent him reeling backward. As he fell, he had that laughable look of surprise and awkward indignity of a man slipping in the bathtub. I heard the dull thud of his fanny hitting the wet tile at poolside. I turned and walked away, glancing over my shoulder, ready to move on him if he got up and started after me. But he seemed disinclined to do anything more than groan and watch me disappear out the gate. Mrs. Nockerman, meanwhile, screamed after me, "You're through, Wolf. I'm having your license revoked. For assault and battery. And I'm suing you for damages."

I kept on walking straight ahead while she raved and screeched like a harpy.

"And keep away from my daughter, you asshole."

Okay, I was fired, the checks would stop coming every week, I owed Freedo twelve grand, and his collection people were probably looking for me. And now there was someone else who'd be happy to see me dead: Tina's mother. It was a long way from symmetry.

42

I flew back to Chicago late the same day. It was dark when Tina picked me up at the airport in a white Jaguar XJ6.

"Nice car," I said, hopping in, tossing my solitary bag and magazines into the backseat.

She leaned across to kiss me. "I missed you, Frank." A huge black stretch limo behind us honked insanely at the delay.

"Screw you," Tina muttered, glaring into the rearview mirror. Then she pulled out into the traffic inching and lurching in the outside lane past the long row of terminals.

I leaned back in the seat and closed my eyes. "Rough trip," I said. "I'm beat."

"Let's go to my place," she said. "Don't look so spooky, Frank, nobody's following me. You'll grab a shower and a nap, then we'll eat and talk." She smiled. "And whatever."

"Can we do the 'whatever' first?"

"Soon as possible," she said. "You like this car? It's Daddy's. He kept it in the garage at his apartment. Should I sell it? I've got my Porsche, but I kind of like this too."

"Aren't you going to ask me about your mother?"

Tina didn't answer. She gunned the engine and the Jag merged effortlessly into the fast-moving traffic beyond O'Hare bound for Chicago. She concentrated silently on her driving, threading the needle again and again between huge trucks at seventy-five m.p.h. If I had been more awake, I might've been nervous.

"Your mother and father were in the dope business together," I said. No sense in beating around the bush, I thought. Might as well tell her everything, quick and simple. I watched her face for a reaction. She stared straight ahead as she raced down the Kennedy Expressway toward the Loop.

"Your mother was—maybe still is—a heavy cocaine user. She says your father forced her to become a mule, a dope carrier. If she didn't play, he'd take away her nose candy. So she ran his packages of flake around the country."

Still no response from Tina.

"Teddy Lane is supposed to be the key to this thing," I continued. "Lane was part of the business. Either he killed your father, or he had him killed. That's what your mother told me. She thinks the cops were too stupid to find that out. And because she didn't want to tell them about her own involvement, she didn't say one word to them."

Without taking her eyes from the road she said, "Teddy killed Daddy? That's insane. Teddy and Daddy were so close. Do you think Mother is trying to frame him?"

"Frame Lane?"

"Yeah, maybe Mother killed Daddy. It's possible, you know. My mother's a rather ruthless person. Nothing she'd do would surprise me."

"She'd need a damn good motive for killing him. You got any ideas about that?"

"No, nothing specific. But maybe you'll find something."

"Your mother tried to bribe me, then fired me."

"I'm not surprised. That's her pattern. She either buys or bullies her way out of things."

"So I'm out of a job, there's no more paycheck, and I owe an Outfit bookmaker twelve thousand bucks."

"All right, you'll drop the case. It's too dangerous anyway. And don't worry about the money you owe. I'll loan it to you and you'll pay them off."

"No, I'm going to keep working on this. It's a matter of principle now. And I'm not going to borrow money from you."

"Then I'll hire you."

"Same rate your mother paid me?"

"Same rate."

"It's a deal."

* * *

She took me to her place and we ate, talked, and whatever. About eleven I called a cab to drive me to my apartment.

"Why go back there," she asked. "It could be dangerous. What if someone's waiting for you? Stay with me tonight."

"I can't. I've got to get an early start tomorrow. I've got questions for Teddy Lane." I also wanted to go home so I could get my guns, but I didn't mention that.

"I wish you'd drop all this, Frank. I don't care anymore who killed Daddy. All that matters is that you're safe."

"It'll all be over soon," I told her.

I had the cabbie circle around the block several times before I was convinced my building wasn't being watched.

I looked into the foyer through the glass door before opening it. The room seemed empty. I came in carefully, ready to move, remembering the bozos who had bushwhacked me there. Nobody waiting for me. And nobody on the stairway.

I opened my apartment door slowly, cautiously, as soundlessly as possible, listening, trying to see in the dark. Nothing in the living room. I went into the bedroom, looked around, opened the closet door, the bathroom, checked under the bed: my .45 automatic and can of Mace were tucked away on the floor exactly where I had left them.

Okay. Nobody was there, and apparently nobody had been there. I undressed without turning on the lights and set my alarm clock for six the next morning. A few moments later I was asleep on the bed in only my shorts.

About three hours later, in the depth of sleep, I felt something cold pushing against my nose. I awoke sweating in the heat to see the face of a gargoyle before me in the dim light that angled in through the bedroom window from the street lamp. It was Watt, shoving the barrel of a huge Magnum under my eyes.

"Don't go for your piece or Mace, hotshot," he said, grinning with satisfaction. "I got 'em already."

"Nice of you to drop in," I said. "My house is your house."

"Shut up, asshole, and get out of bed. Slowly, now, slowly."

As I swung out of bed, he backed away, his gun still on

me. I stood before him in my jockey briefs, barefoot, bare chested, trying to figure some moves to get me out of this.

"You in this for yourself, Watt? Or are you working for somebody?"

"Hey, dip-shit, I said shut up. Just tell me where's your report on the Nockerman case."

"There is no report. My client didn't want one."

With his free hand he threw a punch that hit me in the mouth. I went to the floor, saw the supernovas going off behind my closed eyes.

"Now, where's the fuckin' report? And don't tell me it's at your office. I've been there."

"It's all up here in my head," I said.

"Fine, then I'll have to go someplace with your fuckin' head."

"Where?"

He motioned with his gun for me to stand up. "Come on, we're going."

I stood up.

"Can I get some clothes?"

"No." He laughed. "It's come-as-you-are."

"Like this?" I looked down with feigned embarrassment at my semi-nakedness. "With my shlong out? You kidding me?"

He laughed again and for a minuscule part of a second threw his head back. At that moment I lunged at him, dived into his mid-section, knocking him backward into the wall as I chopped on his right hand. He dropped the gun. I kicked it away and it skittered across the bare floor into the living room.

I tried to grab him by the throat. He brought up his knee and clipped me in the nuts. I went down in agony. He scrambled in a crouch into the living room after the gun.

I went after him, thinking: *What the hell did he do with my .45 and Mace?*

He was about to grab the gun when I jumped on his back with both feet. The air went out of him with a noisy *whoosh*. But he bucked like a bronc and threw me off.

I struggled to my feet. He stood facing me now, knees somewhat bent, arms outspread before him like a knife fighter. He started circling to my right, my bad side where I couldn't defend or attack as well as I could to my left. The more he moved to my right, the more I felt the awkwardness, like a left-handed shortstop. But I inched along with him, moving as he moved, so he couldn't gain on my flank.

I put my head down and lunged at him like a ram. I hit him low, in the pubis. The blow shoved him backward, but not down. I swung my right fist up from the ground and hit him in the testicles. He doubled over, groaning. I chopped at his kidneys right and left with both hands. No apparent effect. He came up again, kicked at my groin, missed. Twisting to the side and stepping back to dodge his foot, I went off balance. He swung at me. I ducked. His hand went past my head, crashed into the wall and through the plaster.

We faced each other, crouching like wrestlers. His eyes kept darting back and forth, from me to his .357 Mag on the floor, then back to me again. I tried to keep in front of the gun so he'd have to go through me to get it. He hissed loudly as he breathed, his bloodshot eyes like boiled eggs in red lacework.

He lunged at my legs. I grabbed a nearby lamp from the table, yanking the cord from the socket as I swung it at his head, shattering the thin ceramic of the base as I connected with his skull. Grunting, he went down.

As he started coming up, I put both my hands together and chopped on the back of his neck. He went down again. I looked quickly behind me for the gun. I couldn't spot it. I wheeled back and kicked him in the face, my bare toes curled under to protect them. I heard the bones of my toes crack as my foot hit his head.

An instant later he was scrambling to his feet, grabbing for my legs. I hit him with a wooden end table. It splintered against his head and shoulders like the break-away furniture in a spaghetti western. He was bleeding profusely now.

He came at me with new ferocity, diving headlong like some quarterback plunging through the line. I sidestepped him, but he still rammed me on the hip. It spilled me on my back, and he was on me instantly, his hands around my windpipe, throttling me as if he were wringing out a wet towel.

I went light-headed with lack of air, thrashed like a manic tarpon, trying to wrench free from the lethal hook. He dripped blood and sweat all over my face. His putrid breath stank like a stagnant swamp. I reached up with one hand

and grabbed the edge of my bookcase, struggled with it, and finally pulled it over on him, all my volumes on astronomy, astrophysics, and the universe crashing down on him like a meteor shower. I felt the heavy bombardment through his body, heard him huff explosively as the wind was knocked out of him. He may have been unconscious for an instant because I squirmed away easily from under his dead weight, and scrambled for the gun.

Before I got it, he fired a shot into the floor right next to me.

I stopped, put my hands up, turned around slowly. He was standing, panting, bleeding like a pig in a slaughterhouse, my own .45 in his hand and pointed at me.

"I should kill you, cocksucker," he said. "But someone wants to see you."

"What a break for me," I said.

"Kick that gun over here."

I kicked the gun across the floor. He bent and picked it up, the .45 still on me.

"Okay, let's go," he said.

We marched through my wrecked living room to the front door.

"Open," he said.

I yanked open the door and it hit him in the head. He reeled backward for a moment. I ran into the hallway and down the stairs.

A moment later I heard Watt flying down the stairs behind me. I ran out of the building. The humid night was fragrant with damp foliage. The sidewalks were empty, bare beneath the feeble yellow light of the tall street lamps.

My feet were scraped raw against the abrasive concrete as I ran. I heard the high-pitched gargling of crickets, the rumbling of an El train a block away, the relentless slap-slap-slapping of Watt's shoes on the sidewalk as he came after me.

I kept a steady thirty-yard lead on him.

I ran into the intersection of Lunt and Greenview. I stood in front of an oncoming car and waved it down. It screeched to a stop. I dashed around and pulled open the door on the passenger side just as the driver was leaning over to lock it.

I jumped in next to the driver. "Someone's chasing me," I said. "Let's get the hell out of here."

The driver was a kid in his twenties. He stared at me, mouth agape, dumbfounded.

"Drive, goddamnit! He's coming after me with a gun."

He floored it and we were out of there.

He looked at me as he drove. "Where's your pants, mister?"

I saw Watt in the rearview mirror as we pulled away. He stood on the corner gasping for air, watching us disappear.

"I'd like you to take me somewhere," I told the young driver. "When we get there, I'll give you some money."

"Sure, mister, sure."

He stopped for a light at Sheridan Road, flung open the door, leaped out of the car, and ran off down the street.

I slid over to the driver's seat and yelled after him, "I'll call you tomorrow, tell you where I left your car."

I drove south down side streets, shirtless and barefoot in my skivvies and nothing else, expecting any instant to be pulled over for indecent exposure in a motor vehicle.

I double-parked on Ashland near Irving, ran into an apartment building where a friend of mine lived, and rang the bell.

A minute or two later I was running up the stairs. My pal, Mickey Polo, was standing in his pajamas on the landing, looking me over like I was crazy.

"Like what the fuck's this? You gone nudist?"

Mickey Polo, bartender, former advertising executive, gun enthusiast. He was forty, thin as an I-beam, with a long, doleful face and gray curly hair cut close to his angular skull.

"Can you loan me some duds?" I asked him.

"I don't hear from you a whole fucking year? Then out of the clear sky you show up in the middle of the night and wanna borrow my best suit?"

"Just give me something to wear till I can get back home."

"I'll see what I got in the closet. The shoes'll be a squeeze, but the rest should fit."

"Thanks, Mick. When I clear this up you get a freebie outfit at Baskin's."

"Write it down and sign it."

"Can I sleep here tonight?"

"Sure. On the couch. But you fix your own breakfast."

"Thanks, Mick. You got my marker now."

"What's going on, Frank? Tell me."

I told him . . . very briefly.

"You think he'll show up here?" Mick asked.

"No chance," I said. "I shook him."

"Yeah? Maybe he'll figure things out and kick my door in."

"How? Nobody knows I ever come up here."

"I hope."

"Can I take your car for a couple hours tomorrow?"

"Sure. I'll leave my keys for you on the hall table. Anything else I can do for you? You got my clothes and my car. Now what else do you want? My apartment, my money, my toothbrush? Just say the word, Frank. Everything I own in the whole world, just consider it yours."

"I want one of your handguns, too, Mick."

"What? Heavy, light?"

"Something big."

"What happened to your own equipment?"

"I think they were taken by this bozo I told you about."

"Okay, Frank. I'll give you my .45. But you drop someone with it, I tell the cops you stole it from me."

"Absolutely. Now, what about the clothes you promised me?"

He went into his bedroom and came back a few moments later with sport jacket, pants, shirt, shoes, and socks.

"You're a beauty, Mick," I told him.

I dressed hurriedly. Everything was a notch too tight, but not bad. I ran back downstairs and hopped into the car. There was no ticket for double-parking. I drove around the corner and parked in the alley behind Mickey's building. Then I went back to his apartment and caught a few hours sleep on the couch.

First thing in the morning, using a source of mine who works for the State of Illinois Motor Vehicle Division, I traced the owner of the car I borrowed through the license number. I called the young man, told him where I had left his Chevy, and thanked him profusely. He was not happy about having been kidnapped.

"Sorry, pal," I told him. "There was a maniac chasing me. I'll mail you the keys and fifty for gas."

I grabbed a shot of O.J. from the refrigerator, hollered good-bye and thanks to the still-sleeping Mickey, and left.

I walked out of the building, down the steps, and from out of nowhere someone threw a full nelson on me.

"My timing's perfect, huh, Frank? I just got here."

He had me from behind and I couldn't see him, but the voice was unmistakable: The Beast, Freedo's collector-enforcer.

"How'd you find me?"

"How'd I find you?"

"Yeah, tell me."

"This is a regular stop of yours when you're hiding out."

"I'm not hiding out," I said.

"Whatever. Freedo says the Man told him you gotta pay what you owe by next Monday. All of it. One hundred percent. You got that?" He gave my head a little shove forward to emphasize his point.

"Where the hell do I get twelve grand in a week?"

"That's your problem, slick. You pay or you're upside down in deep shit." He tightened his grip. "You got that, Wolf?"

"I got it."

He released me. I turned around, my neck a little stiff from the stretch.

"Tell Freedo I want to talk to him."

"You tell him. But be sure to have the money."

"I'll have it," I said. "But not next Monday."

"Good." The Beast smiled, a thin, raptorial leer. "I hope you come up short so's I can bust your fucking head."

"Never happen, Cro-Mag."

He shoved a blunt index finger against my chest to punctuate his warning, poked me several times so hard I felt the vibes ripple through my sternum down to my coccyx. "Just have the money. . . ." He gave me a final poke for good measure, then turned and walked briskly down the street to the curb where he had parked his car, got in and drove away.

I went around to the alley, found Mickey's car, and took off in search of Lane.

43

I drove downtown to LaSalle Street, parked in a city garage and walked a few blocks through the early morning crowds to the Board of Trade building. There was a large group clustered around the entrance, farmers protesting the low price of wheat, corn, other commodities. They wore denim overalls and billed caps from John Deere and Harvester. One man sat atop a tall yellow Cat tractor with giant wheels shouting into a bullhorn about speculators who manipulate the price of grain to the detriment of helpless farmers who were going bankrupt and losing their farms. Another man carried a sign that said: "Don't Kill the Dream." A television news crew with minicam hovered nearby, filming for the six o'clock newscast. A police line held back spectators.

I pushed through the throng and into the building. The place was already swarming with the people who make the markets tick. I took the elevator to Lane's office. There was a new, young receptionist at the desk, smily, friendly.

"I've got an urgent message for Mr. Lane," I told her.

"Well, Mr. Lane called just a few minutes ago and said he'd go right to the pits instead of coming into the office first, as he usually does."

"What time will he get there?"

"When the market opens. About an hour from now. We can contact him on the floor if you like."

"I'll go to the floor myself. What pit will he be in?"

"Soybeans, probably. That's where he usually starts. Mr. Lippert will be here soon. Maybe he can help you."

"Who's Mr. Lippert?"

"Mr. Lane just hired him. He's the new office manager."

"I'll be back to talk to him if I don't find Mr. Lane."

I took the elevator down to the lobby, bought both newspapers, then went to the cafeteria to grab some coffee.

I got my breakfast, sat down in a back booth, and dove into the sports pages. By the time I surfaced again, the markets had already opened. I took the elevator to the trading floor. I heard the distant roar of the open outcry as I stepped out—the sound of the crowd at a major league baseball game. I came to the great portal that gave on the huge trading room and was stopped by a security guard. I took out my wallet and flashed him my Cook County Deputy Sheriff's badge.

"Official business," I said.

"You going to bust someone on the floor?"

"No, just talk to a guy."

"Okay, go in."

"Thanks," I said. "Which one's the soybean pit?"

"Over there." He pointed.

I walked onto the trading floor. The chamber was cavernous, three stories high. The noise was dense and unrelenting, the clamor of a nasty audience at the circus maximus. The floor was crammed with runners bearing buy and sell orders to the pits, brokers and employees of the exchange crisscrossing back and forth from one trading ring to another. Everyone wore jackets, mandatory dress on the floor. High above, on the walls at either end of the room, stretched the long electronic display board. For an instant the place reminded me of those huge wire rooms my father took me to when I was a kid.

The trading pits were high wooden octagons with steps descending to the floor in the center. Traders occupied every level from top to bottom. They jumped and screamed about convulsively, fingers and fists thrust aloft to indicate price, signaling with palms out to sell, palms in to buy.

I threaded my way through the crush of people to the soybean pit, searching through the crowd on every step and station of the octagon for Lane. I didn't see him. I circled the ring slowly, looking at every face. Then, I saw him. At the topmost level, gesturing wildly with his arms.

I waved at him and called his name. He didn't hear me. I climbed up the steps of the ring, trying to shove through the wall of traders. It was like plunging through a scrimmage line.

Suddenly, Lane spotted me. He dropped his arms to his sides, looked at me for a split-second, then ran down the steps on the opposite side of the ring. I scrambled after him in broken-field pursuit through hordes of people wandering everywhere across the floor, bumping into four or five, knocking down two or three.

I caught up with Lane on the far side of the room beneath the price board. I lunged at him like an NFL lineman, tackled him at the legs, and brought him down hard.

Two uniformed security cops were on top of us by then. I flashed my deputy sheriff's badge again as I got up.

"Do you need some assistance?" one of them asked.

"No, thank you," I said. "I can manage."

"We can phone for some backup."

"That won't be necessary, thanks."

They backed away a few feet and watched as Lane stood up and dusted himself off.

"Why'd you run?" I asked Lane.

"Why'd you chase me?" He was panting and sweating like a jogger after a snappy 10K workout.

"Someone wants to kill you," I said.

He blanched. "Who?"

"Joey Watt."

Lane's eyes went blank. "Joey *who*?"

"Watt."

"I don't know the man. Why's he want to kill me?"

"Who knows. You're on his hit list."

"You're bullshitting me."

"I'm telling you the truth." I was lying, of course.

"How do you know?"

"Believe me, I know."

The roar of the trading continued, the traders oblivious to everything but their buying and selling.

44

The much-vaunted intelligence of the criminal mind is a myth. True, there are wizards and near-genius miscreants in every racket. But generally, beyond their specialty, most thugs know nothing about everything, and so your average criminal is a Renaissance ignoramus. They're not too good at logic, either.

So when I returned with Lane to my office, I was fairly confident that Watt wouldn't be watching the place. He'd figure I wouldn't come back here for a while. So he wouldn't either.

Just in case, I had Mick's .45 drawn when I opened the door.

The place had been ransacked—Watt told me he had been here looking for my nonexistent report on the Nockerman case. Everything was upside down and inside out, papers strewn about, file cabinets and desks flipped over, couches and chairs ripped open like disemboweled animals. It was the usual sickening mess you find after sloppy people conduct a systematic search.

"Looks like a landfill," I said.

I took a quick survey of the damage. My camera and tape recorder were smashed and useless. My guns were gone, and so was my small safe. No doubt Watt took it all with him and cracked open the safe elsewhere. There was nothing in it he could use.

"Let's get out of here," Lane said. "The place is creepy."

"Sit down," I said. "I got something to show you."

I lifted my overturned desk and sat behind it. Lane picked up a chair and sat facing me.

Then I showed him my photographs of Watt and his associate.

He looked. "Yeah, so? Who are they?"

"One guy's Joey Watt," I said.

"Means nothing to me."

"The man's going to kill you."

"Kill me? What the hell for? I don't know this guy."

I leaned a little heavier on the bluff. "I broke into Watt's apartment," I said. "He had notes on your daily routine, every move you make."

"He had my schedule?"

"Every move. By the half-hour."

Lane took another look at the photographs.

"Complete strangers to me," he said.

"Don't be a fool, Lane," I told him. "I know what kind of business you were in with Nockerman. Either the cops get you, or this guy does. You want to live? Then talk to me. When we're done, I'll personally escort you to the police. They'll book you, but they'll protect you. Later, you'll make your deal with the feds and go into the Witness Protection Program. Otherwise, you walk the streets and take your chances."

Lane unclenched his teeth, his face relaxed.

"All right, Wolf," he said. "I got to call my office first. I got some live positions in the market and I want to get out."

He punched up his number and spoke into the phone. "Jean, I had to leave the floor unexpectedly this morning. I was long fifty soybean contracts. Sell it all at market price. Soon as possible. Call me here when you get confirmation on the trade." He gave my telephone number and hung up.

Turning to me then, he shrugged; the look on his face said he was ready to talk. "Well?"

I showed him the pictures of Watt and the stranger again. "Who is this man?" I pointed to Watt.

"Joey Watt," Lane said. "He works for a big independent coke dealer named Francisco Rotunda. Watt's a killer and a collector. He was also a go-between from Rotunda to Nockerman. Yeah, that's right, Nockerman and Rotunda did a lot of business together. Rotunda was Nockerman's main supplier."

"Who's the other guy?"

"Vince Crucerosa. Rotunda's right hand. He's also Rotunda's nephew, but he's really like a son to the old man."

"Why would Watt want to kill you?"

"Rotunda probably ordered it. The feds came to see me. Asked a lot of questions and said they'd be back. I was told the federal grand jury is getting ready to call me. I swore to Rotunda I wouldn't talk, but I guess he doesn't trust me."

"Is that why Nockerman was killed?"

"Yeah."

"Did Watt kill him?"

"Rotunda ordered it. Watt pulled the trigger."

"How do you know?"

"I heard them talking about it. I was there when they planned it. I also heard them talk about blowing away Angler and Osvald. Right after they hit Nockerman."

"Why the hell would they talk about hitting Nockerman in your presence?"

"To scare me shitless. It worked, too, take my word."

"Why'd they want to hit Nockerman?"

"Because Rotunda was afraid Nockerman would spill to the grand jury. Plus Nockerman was getting an attitude problem. Even at his sanest, Nocky was crazy."

I nodded in agreement.

Lane continued, "But he got even worse. He made a load of money when the stock market crashed. Says he saw it coming weeks in advance, so he bought put options. He was short everything, all the majors, IBM, GM, you name it. And he bought the bear side of the S & P index. So the big collapse comes, he makes out like a bandit. He was going to use the money to go bigger into the dope business, strictly for himself this time, without Rotunda as a partner, maybe even muscle into Rotunda's markets."

"Did Rotunda know about Nocky's plans?"

"Yeah."

"How?"

"Well, I told him."

"Why?"

"I was afraid Rotunda would find out what Nocky wanted to do, think I was part of it, and have us both killed."

"Why did he think Nockerman would talk to the grand jury and implicate himself?"

"Because Rotunda knew Nocky was nuts and unpredictable. And he figured Nocky might make some kind of deal for himself if he rolled over on his partners."

"So Rotunda was just hedging his bets?"

"Yeah."

"Tell me what happened the night Nockerman was killed."

"Rotunda set up a coke buy at Nocky's apartment. Told him to have three million cash for his end of the deal. Plan was for Rotunda, Vince Crucerosa, and Watt to go to Nocky's place and pretend to wait for the Colombians to show. When the chance came up, Watt would make the hit."

"Just like that? Right there in the apartment?"

"Rotunda figured the cops would think it was a dope-related murder, which it was, and not run after it too hard. 'Course, Rotunda also planned to grab Nocky's three mill for himself. Which he did."

"And that's how it went down?"

"Apparently," Lane said.

"What happened next?"

"The following day Vince called me and said Mr. Rotunda wanted to talk to me. Watt and Vince came for me in the car. We drove up to Rotunda's place on the North Shore. Rotunda was waiting for us in his den. There was food and drink, like a party or something. Rotunda was very gracious. How nice of me to come on such short notice, he said. Have a bite of this and that, have some wine, some coffee, whatever I want. You know, the typical Latin American multimillionaire playing host. Then he tells me Nockerman is dead, very matter-of-fact, like it means nothing to him."

"Okay, then what?"

"Then Rotunda brings out Nockerman's attaché case. I recognized it right away. He opened it up and I saw that it was crammed full of money. Big bills, too, no tens and twenties. He counted out four hundred thousand and laid it before me on a coffee table. 'Here,' he said to me. 'This is for you. You'll set up a new washing machine for us. Entirely new people—' "

"What are you talking about? What kind of washing machine?"

"Nockerman was running a money-laundering operation through his brokerage firm."

"Besides the dope business?"

"Yeah. Washed his own money and Rotunda's, and a lot of other people's. Millions. Charged a fat commission too. It adds up, believe me."

"Okay, you'll tell me about it later. Get back to Rotunda."

Lane continued. "So Rotunda tells me to set up a new wash with new people. When he says new people, I figured something happened to the old people. Well, it hadn't happened yet, but it was going to happen—Angler and Osvald would be dead as Nockerman within a few days."

"Angler and Osvald were part of the wash?"

"They were the key people, along with Nockerman. Anyway, Rotunda tells me he's going to buy Nockerman's brokerage house and I'm going to front it. I'll be a full partner, he tells me, and run things just like Nockerman, including the washing machine. But Rotunda warns me not to say anything. Otherwise, he says, he'll have my daughter killed first, then me."

I knew then why Lane believed me when I told him Watt was going to kill him.

"And Rotunda never makes an idle threat," Lane said. "He tells you he'll do something, it's in the bank. So when he threatens my daughter and me, I believe him. Only problem was, I couldn't set up the new wash overnight."

"Why not? You already had a successful wash."

"With Angler and Osvald dead, the key men were gone. I needed time to get the right people and put the new machinery in place. Nockerman did it originally years ago by giving Angler and Osvald deliberately bum tips in the market. Strung 'em along beautifully at first, let 'em win a lot of money. Then they came in heavier and lost their asses. Nocky carried 'em for months, and when they wound up owing him hundreds of thousands in margin, Nocky had 'em by the balls."

"And that's how he got them involved in the wash?"

"Yeah. Then they started making so much money, Nocky had 'em hooked."

"Did Watt kill them?"

"Yeah."

"How do you know?"

"I told you, I heard Watt talk about it. Rotunda ordered the hits."

"Why were they killed?"

"Same reason Nockerman was killed. The feds were on their case and Rotunda didn't trust them to keep quiet."

"Why didn't they want you hit earlier, when all this federal heat first came down?"

"Like I said, they needed me to set up the new wash. And of course, the feds hadn't gotten to me yet. But now that the government's wise to me, I guess I'm no longer indispensable."

"Did Watt torch Angler's garage?"

"Yeah."

"Why?"

"It had all the computer equipment in it that Angler used to alter the clearinghouse records for the wash. There was also a lot of incriminating stuff on disks and so forth. Watt didn't know from nothing about computers, so he burned the whole place."

"Who's Lippert?"

"New guy at the office. Vince sent him to me. He knows the commodity business inside out. Sharp enough to run the brokerage firm and the wash good as Nockerman, if he ever sets it up. I assume he's Rotunda's hand-picked replacement for me."

"Tell me about the wash. How does it work?"

"It's ingenious. Almost foolproof. Nocky dreamt it up himself. I'll give you the bare bones, without the details."

"Good. Business confuses me. Talk slowly too."

"The wash is based on fake commodity trades. Nocky doctored them to look profitable, so that dope profits are disguised as market profits. The bogus trades are all back-dated and entered into the records so there's a paper trail which makes everything look legal. And it's all based on real market action. Let's say silver was six bucks last year and ten this year. Nockerman fixes a trade to look like you bought it at six and sold it at the top. He cooks the records, writes the back-dated checks, handles all the paperwork. Then Angler back-enters the data into the clearinghouse computer. He did it from his garage, didn't even have to be at work. He had a device that could access the clearinghouse computer and transmit information over the phone. Now Os-

vald comes in. He back-dates the accounts and computer
records at the bank, and doctors the government reporting
requirements log—you know, the law about reporting every
transaction of ten thousand dollars or more. Then Osvald
issues a check to the clearinghouse, and Angler arranges for
a clearinghouse check to be issued to Nockerman. Finally,
Nockerman writes a check to the lucky shooter who apparently made the big killing in the market. The money is
drawn from Nockerman's account at Osvald's bank. The guy
who gets the money reports it to the IRS as profit from commodity market speculation. It's money he made selling dope,
of course, but he pays his tax and everybody's happy. Nice,
huh?"

"Yeah, damn nice," I said. "Three people are dead. And
you're probably next."

Lane ignored my remark and said, "And the beautiful
thing is that nobody at the bank or the clearinghouse knew
anything about this—just Angler and Osvald."

"Nobody else was in on it?"

"Not a soul."

"One more thing," I said. "What happened to Arcana on
that boat down in Florida?"

"You know about that?"

"Not as much as you do. Tell me."

"Nockerman killed him."

"Why?"

"Because Nockerman was a fucking lunatic. Even before
he started on coke. But once he got on that nose candy, he
went ape. Eventually, he became a free-baser. He got para-
noid, like they all get. You couldn't talk to him. A real maniac. Finally, he wound up killing people."

And God knows what else, I thought.

"So we went to Florida on a dope deal," Lane said. "Our
first. Nocky needed money, so did I. We were partners, but I
was only in for a small piece. Nocky had set up the deal with
Arcana. I didn't know you in those days, Wolf, but I remember Nocky hired you to see if Arcana had mob connections.
He didn't. Anyway, we're supposed to rendezvous with another boat a few miles off the Florida coast and take delivery
of the coke. Supposed to be good stuff, from Colombia by way
of Cuba. Arcana was the go-between in the deal. So we meet
the boat and they load on the dope. Just a couple small over-

night bags. Nockerman takes a look at the stuff then starts arguing about something in Spanish with these people. I don't know the language, so I don't know what the hell's going on. But I was on deck, and I saw the whole thing. Everyone's yelling at each other. Suddenly Nockerman pulls a gun and shoots the two Colombians. The boat they came in revs up and speeds away. Then Arcana starts screaming at Nockerman. So Nocky squeezes off two and Arcana goes down. He walks up to Arcana, gives him a kick, then heaves him over the side. 'Nobody fucks me,' says Nocky. 'Nobody.' Then we threw over the two Colombians. I was scared shitless. But I didn't know what to do. We cleaned up the deck and cruised around a little, trying to figure out our next moves. Then a heavy storm comes up and starts tossing us around. Almost sinks us. Which is a lucky break, because now we can tell the authorities Arcana was washed overboard. So we cooked up a story and came back. A few days later there was a brief inquest, and the case was closed. Accidental death."

"Why'd you stay with Nockerman all those years? You knew he was crazy, you knew he was a killer?"

"I stayed with him because of the money. You ever have real money, Wolf? The kind of money that changes your life? I've got it and believe me, you don't know what it's like until you have it yourself. You can tell the whole world 'fuck you.' Wolf, listen to me, help me get out of this. Help me get away from these bastards and from the cops and I'll give you four hundred grand."

I laughed.

"Listen to me, Wolf," he pleaded. "I don't want to go into this fucking witness program. I don't want to spend the rest of my life in some one-horse town in New Mexico. I'll give you four hundred grand. Up front, cash, no taxes. Relax, travel, buy some property, live like a gentleman. Four hundred grand, Wolf. In a half hour I'll put it in your hands. Come on, we'll go together. I'll get it right now."

"Four hundred thousand? Cash?"

"Yes. You'll have it in thirty minutes."

"Damn tempting," I said. Must be my lucky week. Everybody wants to buy me off.

"Think of it, Wolf, no more 'yes sir, no sir, may I kiss

your ass, sir?' You'll be rich, and everyone else can get fucked."

"I'm not interested," I said.

"You want more money? All right, you've got it."

As Lane talked I heard someone come into the entrance hall downstairs. I put my left index finger to my lips in a signal for him to keep quiet. With my other hand, I took the gun that Mickey had given me out of my belt and leveled it at the door.

I listened for footsteps on the stairs. I heard two people quietly ascending the steps. Then they were in the corridor outside my office. I heard the key turn in the lock, and they came into my anteroom. I pulled the hammer back on the .45.

A moment later my inner office door came crashing in, the glass shattering in a thousand fragments. Watt and the man who had been with him at the hotel stood before us, both with guns drawn and pointed at me and Lane.

"Come on in," I said.

Lane went white as cottage cheese.

"You shouldn't have left this phone number with your secretary," I told him.

It would've been the right time to signal Hershey at the deli down the street with my under-the-desk alarm system, but when they had flipped my desk over, they yanked the wires out. Besides, I never did bother to replace the wornout batteries.

Watt and his partner, the man Lane had identified in my photographs as Vince Crucerosa, kept their guns on me. Slowly, inch by inch, they fanned out in opposite directions until they stood at almost right angles to me.

I kept my .45 at arm's length, moving my aim back and forth first to one, then the other.

Watt said, "Put the gun down, Wolf. You shoot one of us, the other'll get you."

Maybe I could squeeze off two rounds fast enough to drop them both. But they were standing too far apart now. I didn't like the odds. I put my gun down on the desk.

Watt laughed, walked over, picked up the gun and put it in his pocket.

"You asking yourself where'd I get the key to get in here? Right on your dresser where you left it, asshole."

"See what they're holding," Vince said.

Watt motioned for us to stand and quickly rubbed us down. Up close his face looked like a piece of wormy wood. His white shirt collar was stained with pancake makeup. He turned to his companion and said, "Nothing on 'em, Vince."

Then Watt saw the photographs of him and Vince on my desk. He picked one up and studied it. "Well, I'll be god-damned. Look at this." He handed them to Vince. Vince glanced at the photos briefly, then laid them back on my desk.

"How'd you know to come after Joey?" he asked me.

"I took a wild guess."

"You keep lousy records," Vince said. "We couldn't find your file on the Nockerman case."

"Can't say you didn't try hard enough."

"All right," Vince said. "Get up. Both of you. We're going to see someone. Joey, take the photographs."

Lane's skin had turned to blue-gray, like a man in the throes of cardiac arrest. "Who we going to see?" he asked.

"Someone you know," said Watt. He was smiling, enjoying Lane's terror.

Why didn't Watt kill me and Lane then and there? And if he didn't kill me, odds are he wasn't the guy who shot at me on the roof. Well, I figured that already when he didn't ice me back in my apartment. Then who the hell wanted me dead? Mrs. Nocky perhaps? Maybe she just wished it; I didn't think she had the guts or motive enough to have it done. So who else could it be? Then, through the process of elimination, I knew beyond a doubt: the bankers! That was a definite *maybe*.

Watt and Vince marched us out and down the stairs, their guns still on us but concealed in their suit jackets. They looked like a pair of Napoleons, Watt to our right, Vince to our left. Outside there was a dark-blue four-door Mercedes sedan double-parked at the curb. The guy at the wheel looked like a teenager. Skinny, Hispanic. Maybe Colombian?

Watt shoved us into the backseat and got in beside us. Vince got into the front and turned around to watch us, gun still in hand.

"Let's go," he said, and the driver took off.

45

We drove north by way of Sheridan Road, passing again that almost interminable stretch of wealth embodied in the opulent dwellings along the lakefront. Nobody uttered a word. Everybody kept looking at one another, including the driver, who eyeballed us in the rearview mirror. Somewhere beyond Lake Forest we turned right onto a private road, then passed through a huge open gate of ornamental iron grillwork and onto a broad, serpentine driveway that cut through an exquisitely maintained greensward.

"Who lives here?" I asked. "Rotunda?"

Nobody answered.

We pulled up before an enormous stone mansion in Italian palazzo style, three stories high, massive in scale, with a cloistered arcade leading from the house into a formal garden.

The place was probably built around the turn of the century, when a million dollars had some real buying power. Watt shoved us out of the car. I smelled the lake nearby and could see the private beach far down at the foot of the bluff.

The driver led the way along a wide flagstone path that curved around to the rear of the house. Watt and Vince walked behind us, their guns in our backs. Lane stumbled once or twice. "I'm getting dizzy," he said. "I think I'm having a heart attack."

His complaint was ignored.

The driver opened the back door with a key and we went into the house, passed through a small mud room, then through a larger room with built-in shelves stocked with all manner of provisions in cans, sacks, and boxes. The driver then disappeared through swinging doors into the kitchen, which seemed big enough to service a restaurant, with stainless steel refrigerators, giant stove, long butcher block tables and counters.

"Down here," Watt ordered, and he shoved us to the right through a broad archway.

We went down a steep flight of stairs to the basement, turned right and walked down a long corridor past a paneled billiard room, then past an extensive wine cellar with rack upon rack of dusty bottles. Then we turned left and walked by several closed doors, then left again.

Finally, we emerged into a large rectangular room that looked like the lobby of a swank hotel, with a thick carpet on the floor and plush leather couches and easy chairs scattered about. Off to the left there was a closed elevator door, further adding to the lobby look.

"Sit down," Watt ordered.

Lane and I sat side by side in a tufted leather sofa. Watt backed away a short distance, a big Mag leveled at us. Vince walked across the room, gun still in hand, picked up a phone from an end table, and poked three numbers.

"Hello, Keeko . . . Yeah, they're here now. We found some photos Wolf took of me and Watt. . . . Front of Watt's hotel . . . Yeah, Wolf took them. . . . I don't know. . . . We'll have to find out."

Vince hung up the phone and looked our way. "Rotunda's coming right down," he said.

Watt said, "Good, I hope we can have some fun." He didn't smile.

I heard a motor click on somewhere in the house, then the slow hum of an elevator—probably Rotunda descending. The noise abruptly stopped and the elevator door opened.

Rotunda. He strode briskly into the room, a tall, girthsome man with a ramrod posture and imperious air. He was dark, Colombian maybe, early fifties, clean-shaven, with black hair slicked back and parted in the middle, 1930s-style. His face was bloated from good food and sedentary living. But he looked dapper in his double-breasted suit of navy blue exquisitely cut in European style, pinched at the waist, shaped at the shoulders, cuffs trimmed high to show lots of linen. He nodded at Watt and Vince. They uttered polite greetings in response. Then Rotunda settled into a voluminous wing chair directly opposite Lane and me, no more than five fee away.

"Let's see the photos," he said.

Vince handed him the prints, which he studied one by one, pursing his lips and uttering a low humming sound. "Well," he said, returning the pictures to Vince, "nothing incriminating here. Just the disturbing knowledge that you know who we are, Mr. Wolf."

Rotunda's voice was deep and resonant, well-cultivated, vaguely foreign with overtones of the Atlantic seaboard, a South American oligarch with an Ivy League education. He held his chin high when he spoke, looking down and past his nose with that arrogance peculiar to aristocrats with plenty of land in one of those countries in which a couple dozen or so families own everything, including the government.

"Our problem now," he continued, "is to determine whom you've told about us. Where have you hidden your file on the Nockerman case?"

"There is no file. My client wanted it that way. I've already told that to your lackies here."

I could've lied and told him that I hid the nonexistent Nockerman file somewhere with instructions to release it to the cops on my death. But what would that accomplish? He'd instruct Watt to twist my arm until I told him where I had stashed it. No percentage.

"Well, then," Rotunda said, "have you mentioned my name to anyone in connection with your investigation? Who knows about me, and what precisely do they know?"

Watt came up behind Rotunda's chair, glowering at me as he awaited my answer.

"I never knew you were involved in this until today," I said. "Mr. Lane here told me."

"Who told you Mr. Watt was associated with us?" Rotunda asked.

"Nobody. I figured it out myself."

"That Angler woman say something about me?" Watt asked.

"Who's that Angler woman?" I asked.

"So my name has not been associated with any unpleasantness?" Rotunda asked.

I said, "What unpleasantness? The murders of Nock-erman, Angler, and Osvald?"

Rotunda threw back his head and laughed, his wattles rippling.

"The Nockerman murder? Well, sir, I had nothing to do with that, believe me. Nor the others, in point of fact. My associates here and I went to Nockerman's apartment some weeks ago on a business matter. About midnight or so, in the middle of our discussion, we heard the front door open unexpectedly. Someone apparently had a key and let themselves in. Nockerman quickly shooed us into another room down the hall, obviously not wanting Vince, Watt, and myself to see his visitor, or vice versa. At any rate, we heard Nock-erman call out to his uninvited guest, 'I'm in the study.'

"Being curious by nature, as we all are, I left the door of our room slightly ajar so I could hear what was happening. I could see nothing, mind you, but I heard a few things. We all did, as a matter of fact.

"We heard her walk into Nockerman's study—yes, it was a woman. Then there was a protracted silence, as if they were kissing and embracing. Then I heard fragments of a murmured conversation, very intimate, it seemed. A moment or two later the unpleasantness began. At first it seemed like a lovers' quarrel. It had that tone; we've all heard it. Then it turned ugly. A terrible argument ensued. Nockerman raised his voice most disagreeably, shouted something about not giving her the money she had coming. I couldn't quite make it out. Suddenly, to our utter amazement, we heard a gunshot. Just one. All was silent for a long time afterward. And then we heard her hurried footsteps across the floor and out the door."

"Why should I believe you?" I asked. "What compelling reason do you have to tell me the truth?"

"None at all. Except my sense of honor as a gentleman."

"Yeah, right. You sure you didn't see the woman?" I had a sudden, disturbing hunch about her identity.

Rotunda shook his head, and went on. "We saw no one. If it were possible, we would've left the apartment through another exit, but we had to pass through Nockerman's study. So we waited a few moments, then cautiously we returned. There he was, on the floor, his head in a pool of blood. Needless to say, we were extremely surprised and upset. Vince took a quick look at Nockerman and determined that he was indeed dead. Naturally we left immediately."

"Why didn't you contact the police?"

Rotunda shrugged. "I'm a man who minds his own business."

"Where was the gun that shot Nockerman?"

"The woman who killed him apparently took it with her."

"Impossible," I said. "Unless she also killed Angler and Osvald." I knew then, or thought I knew, what had happened that night. "By the way," I said, "who took Nocky's three million?"

Rotunda frowned, his fleshy lips puckered. He muttered something to Watt.

Watt walked up to me and slapped my face, back and forth with the flat of his hand, four, five, six times. I squeezed my eyes shut, felt the hot sting, saw the whirling pinwheels and exploding rockets in the dark. When I opened my eyes again, Watt had backed away and now stood at Rotunda's right side.

Shrugging, and smiling slightly, almost benignly, Rotunda said, "You haven't been very forthcoming with us, Mr. Wolf. I'll have to ask Mr. Watt here now to apply his boot to your ass. In a manner of speaking, that is."

Watt chuckled. "I'd like that," he said.

"You see, Mr. Wolf," Rotunda said, "I am forced by circumstances to do these distasteful things, which run contrary to my true nature. Not a happy choice," he shrugged again, "but I must survive."

"Why should a cockroach like you survive?"

"Because survival is the first law of nature. One uses whatever means lie at hand. Speaking of which, your government wants to destroy me. There's an unconstitutional law or two on the books. RICO, and the Narcotics Forfeiture Act. Which simply means that your government can seize my assets if they are thought to be derived from the sale of narcotics or racketeering. Well, Mr. Wolf, I have no intention of letting the U.S. government steal from me everything I've worked so hard to obtain. In fact, I'm prepared to kill to prevent such piracy."

"Which means eventually you'll have to kill Watt and Vince too," I said.

Watt and Vince glared at me.

Rotunda answered quickly. "Utter nonsense. Vince is like my own son, so I'd hardly expect him to betray me. And Mr. Watt is a professional. He respects the confidentiality of his clients. Just as you do, Mr. Wolf."

Abruptly, Rotunda rose from his chair, tilting his head back with aristocratic hauteur. "Vince," he called, "see just how much Mr. Wolf knows about our affairs, and who he's told about them. Then take him and Mr. Lane for a ride in the country."

Rotunda moved toward the elevator.

I knew then I was going to die if I didn't do something. I stopped thinking. As Rotunda crossed in front of me I leaped at him, throwing my arm around his fat neck in a stranglehold and maneuvering myself behind him. With my other hand I grabbed his arm and twisted it behind his back. He groaned in pain. He was all flab, but stronger than I expected. But I had him now as a shield from his gunmen.

Watt and Vince both raised their guns, extended them arm's length in my direction.

"Go ahead, shoot," I taunted them. "You'll put holes in your boss here and let all the air out of him."

I pulled Rotunda back slowly toward the couch, moving in front of Lane. Watt and Vince turned slowly on their heels to follow me with their guns as if tracking with a camera.

"Lane," I said, "stand up and get behind me."

"I can't," he whimpered, "they'll kill me."

"Get up, goddamnit, Lane. This is your only chance."

He rose slowly, like a man who ached in every joint, then moved behind me.

"Stay right behind me now, Lane," I said. "We're going to the elevator."

I backed Rotunda toward the elevator step by step, my arm still around his neck, my other hand twisting his arm. Lane was behind us. Watt started to circle around to my right, his gun still fixed on me, as Vince watched impassively.

"Back off, Watt," I ordered, squeezing Rotunda's neck with my arm. "I'll strangle this fat bastard."

Rotunda gasped and sputtered. "I can't breathe."

We got to the elevator.

"Open the door," I told Lane.

He opened it. We backed in. I was oozing sweat from every pore.

Rotunda yelped, "Get me out of this, Vince."

Vince and Watt watched helplessly as the door to the elevator closed.

I asked Rotunda, "What's on the top floor?"

"Ballroom."

"Hit that button, Lane."

The car jerked, then moved up slowly.

I pulled my arm hard against Rotunda's neck. "You got a gun on you?"

"Inside left breast pocket."

I tightened my stranglehold until I heard him gasp, then with my other hand I reached into his jacket and lifted the gun. It was a .32 automatic. I put the barrel against his head.

"What else you got on you?"

"Nothing," he said.

I gave him a quick rubdown with my free hand. He was clean.

"Who else is in the house here besides the driver?"

"Nobody."

Lane said, "Why we going to the top floor? Let's get off and make a break for it."

"You mean run through this barn like blind mice looking for an exit? While Rotunda's boys pick us off?"

"Let's take Rotunda with us as a hostage," Lane said. "He'll lead us out of here."

"Too risky, not worth the gamble. Anyway, the man's too fat. He can't run fast enough. And if it looks like we're getting away, his boys'll get scared and shoot right through him."

"I got to get out of here, Wolf," Lane whimpered. "I don't feel well. I got chest pains. I think I'm having a heart attack. Is my face turning blue?"

"You look fine."

The elevator stopped suddenly. Third floor. The ballroom.

Lane opened the door.

"Hold it open," I told him. I let go of Rotunda and pointed the gun at him. "Now, Mr. Rotunda, take off your clothes. Shoes and socks too."

Rotunda glared at me. "This is positively perverse," he proclaimed.

He huffed and wheezed as he stripped, leaving his clothing in a pile at his feet.

"Lane," I said, "take that stuff and jam the elevator door so that it won't close."

We stepped into the ballroom. It was a wide, rectangular chamber, maybe sixty feet long, a wall of mirrored panels on one side, a series of French doors on the other, which gave on a broad outdoor terrace that ran the entire length of the room. The floors were oak parquet. At the far end was a small stage with a grand piano on it. There was gilded plaster and carved woodwork of incredibly baroque complexity everywhere. And over it all arched a vaulted ceiling from which hung several chandeliers, and which was covered with murals of plump cherubs cavorting in sylvan groves. Just like the Sun King's gallery of mirrors at Versailles.

Rotunda turned to face me. He stood now in sleeveless undershirt and monogrammed silk boxer shorts of nacreous white. His flesh was a mottled, sickly pink, his chubby bare legs slightly bowed. "You see what wealth I possess, Mr. Wolf?"

"Yeah . . . How else can a person get up here besides the elevator?"

"I want to make you a business proposition," Rotunda said. "I can give you cash, negotiable securities, arrange for a secret account to be opened in your name. Switzerland, or the Bahamas."

"You look ridiculous talking high finance in your skivvies," I said.

"I fail to see the humor here. I'm an old man, Wolf, I'm ill, I don't want to spend my last years in prison. I'll pay anything. Name it. How much?"

"How do people get up here besides the elevator?"

He answered impatiently, angry, frustrated; I wasn't snapping at his bait. "There's a stairway at the other end, opposite the bandstand."

"That's all? No service elevators or anything?"

"No, that's it. Now, Wolf, please, let's reason this thing out together. I can give you a future of ease and comfort. More money than you ever had in your life. And all the power that comes with it. That's the sweetest of all, Wolf, the power."

I studied his face. He looked back at me, wide-eyed, hopeful, sweating with the effort of trying to buy me.

"What'll you give me?"

"One million, American."

I didn't answer right away. I glanced at Lane, then back to Rotunda.

"I want five million," I said.

"Five million?" Rotunda sputtered. "You, sir, are a thief."

"And you, sir, are my prisoner. And soon you will be a prisoner of the state."

Rotunda smiled. "You shall have your five million, Mr. Wolf. And in return I shall have my freedom, along with Mr. Lane here."

"No, Wolf. Don't sell me out," Lane pleaded. "He'll kill me."

"Utter nonsense," Rotunda said.

"How will the money be paid?" I asked Rotunda.

"You'll be paid in any manner you desire," Rotunda said. He was beaming with satisfaction.

"I want U.S. dollars in a Swiss bank account."

"Easily done, Mr. Wolf. Easily."

"I bet."

Rotunda looked at me, hopeful, anticipating.

"You're going to jail, Mr. Rotunda."

"How's that? I don't understand you."

"I don't want your money," I said.

"Don't want my money?"

"No."

"Let me understand this," he said. "You are refusing a fee of five million American to let me go?"

"You got it."

"I don't understand people like you," Rotunda said, shaking his head in sad amazement. "Nothing means anything to you. You have no values, you have no ambitions, you have no grand vision of the future. What are you, Wolf? A fool, a psychopath? What?"

"I don't know what I am. But I know what you are. Everything you touch dies."

"I'll tell you what you are, Mr. Wolf," he said. "You are a

very ignorant and unworldly man. Not the sort that compre-
hends what one can do with five million Yankee dollars."

"You're probably right. Is there a phone up here?"

"No."

"What are those doors on either side of the bandstand?"

"Toilets and a dressing room for the band, and a little
service kitchen," he said.

"What about a fire escape?"

"There's no other way out," Rotunda said. "So unless we
make a deal, sooner or later my people will kill you. They'll
starve you out, you can't get away. Wolf! You're not one of
those misguided idealists who would rather die than—"

I interrupted before he could finish. "I would rather live.
Now shut up and move. You, too, Lane."

They moved in a slow procession across the polished
parquet floor, breaking through beam after beam of bright
sunlight, which angled in through the windows, their images
reflected in the mirrors as they passed. Even in his under-
wear and bare feet, Rotunda moved with regal aplomb. Lane
stumbled along muttering complaints about his aches and
pains.

We came to the stage. I gave a couple sharp yanks on the
cord that drew the curtains and a length of it came falling
down. I gathered it up and marched Rotunda and Lane
through the door on the left and into the bathroom. I tied
them up hand and foot, back to back. When they were well
secured, I set my gun down out of reach, made them lie on
the floor facing in opposite directions and fanny to fanny,
and finished tying them with tight square knots.

I went out to the ballroom to wait. Watt and Vince would
be coming after me soon.

I climbed up on the stage and rolled the piano bench
around behind the broad side of the piano and got on it so
that my feet and legs couldn't be seen by anyone coming into
the room from the stairway. I looked at my watch. I waited.

After a while, my legs started to cramp.

A few minutes later I heard it: a squeaking noise from
the kitchen. The sound was familiar. I tried to place it.

Finally, it clicked: the sound of a pulley that needed oil.
A dumbwaiter! In the kitchen.

I got up slowly, and in a crouch with gun ready came
down from the stage, quiet, without haste, with an eye on

the stairway in case they were coming at me from two fronts at once.

The sound stopped. So did I. Then it started again. I moved to the door, opened it. The kitchen was small, a sink, stove, and refrigerator; enough space and equipment to serve hors d'oeuvres and champagne.

On the right wall near the sink was the door to the dumbwaiter. Closed. The squeaking began again. Someone coming up. The noise stopped. I ducked. The door opened cautiously.

It was Rotunda's driver, gun in hand, folded into the small space knees to chest like a fetus. He saw me and was startled, jerked his arm up and shot, missing. An instant later I fired once, hitting him just below the neck. He slumped, dropped the gun, his shirt suddenly red and wet. The look on his face was not surprise, it was resignation. I had a hunch they'd send this poor bastard up against me first.

I went over and felt his pulse. There wasn't any. I picked up his gun, a .22 Ruger 8-shot automatic, a piece much in favor with professional hit men. I flicked on the safety and shoved the gun into my pants.

I opened the kitchen door a sliver and came out by centimeters, wary, hardly breathing.

I heard Rotunda yelling from the bathroom. "Wolf, are you alive? What happened? Wolf, damn you, answer me."

I didn't answer. I went back to the bench behind the piano. I could peek over the top toward the stairway directly opposite and had a clear view. If they were going to come after me, Watt and Vince would have to walk up those stairs.

Rotunda screamed out again, "Wolf, are you there? Your Mr. Lane blacked out. He's had a heart attack. He's dying. You've got to give him mouth to mouth. I'm in no position to do it myself." Rotunda laughed. Then there was silence. Then, "Wolf, did you hear me. A man is dying."

That's when I saw their inverted reflection in the crystal facets of the furthest chandelier, which hung at the entrance to the ballroom—Watt and Vince in miniature, hundreds of them upside down, mirrored in the polished glass as they climbed the staircase, guns drawn.

I crouched down on the bench behind the piano, my legs up.

It was dark on stage, and I was able to watch from behind the piano as they approached, the raised lid casting a deep shadow, which further concealed me from view.

Watt and Vince came to the head of the stairs, split like a forked tongue to flatten themselves against the ballroom walls, Watt to my left along the mirrors, Vince to my right along the French doors. They advanced like point men on a recon patrol in the heart of Nam, slowly, soundlessly, eyes continually scanning.

Why didn't they get in their cars and drive away from all this, instead of coming up here to kill or be killed? Were they like me? I don't have to win, but I have to play.

They were closing in on me, well within range of my automatic. I ducked behind the piano. I could see Watt's feet and their mirrored reflection. Vince was on the other side, across the dance floor near the windows. I couldn't see him, but I felt his presence.

Rotunda might have sensed it, too; he suddenly bellowed, "I'm tied up in the bathroom. Can you hear me? Wolf is out there waiting for you."

Vince yelled, "He's behind the piano."

Watt fired blindly in my direction.

I lunged to my left onto the floor from behind the piano, still partially shielded by the bulk of the instrument, and fired down at a slight angle, one, two, three shots into Watt before he could blink in disbelief, the slugs boring right through him and shattering the mirrors, flakes and fragments of glass noisily falling like a cascade of ice. Watt went down like a puppet whose strings had been cut.

At the same time, Vince had opened on me, firing in a panic with wild inaccuracy, hitting the piano, *thump, thump, thump,* the wood splintering, steel strings snapping, flying, and twanging, the sound like crazy banjo music.

Still on the floor, I turned toward Vince, squeezed off three more shots, which missed him, shattering the glass panels in the French door behind him. He pulled open what was left of the door, backed onto the terrace, fired a second volley, *ploom, ploom, ploom, ploom,* the slugs punching holes in the boards where I lay. I fired the final shot from the .32, missing him again. I pulled out the Ruger then, flicked off the safety, fired three times. He was hit, dropped his gun, staggered backward clutching his stomach, bumped against the terrace railing, then fell forward on his face. Even at some distance from the man I knew he was dead.

I got up, still holding the Ruger, came down from the stage and walked through the ballroom to the stairs, Rotunda howling from the bathroom, "Who's out there? Vince? Wolf?" I didn't answer, and I didn't stop to look at the two men I had killed.

I found a phone in the master bedroom on the second floor and called the Lake County Sheriff's police. I told them to bring an ambulance along.

I went back upstairs and into the bathroom where I had left Rotunda and Lane. When I walked in Rotunda asked, "Is Vince dead?"

"Yeah," I said quietly.

Rotunda muttered something in Spanish that sounded like a prayer and began sobbing loudly. *"Mi hijo, mi hijo."*

I asked Lane, "You okay?"

He nodded.

"The man here said you had a heart attack."

"Asthma," Lane said. "I'm feeling a little better now."

"Me too," I said.

46

As I stood outside on the terrace of Rotunda's ballroom I heard the sirens howling far away and drawing closer. A few minutes later a brigade of squad cars and meat wagons pulled into the driveway, mars lights flashing.

"Up here," I called, as cops and medics leaped from their vehicles and converged on the house. "It's all over."

Rotunda and Lane were taken into custody on my say-so —cops tend to believe a licensed P.I. in good standing.

I spent most of the day until late afternoon in the Lake County Sheriff's office explaining things to the captain in command. I told him the whole story, but I left out a few parts, including Rotunda's allegation that some unknown woman killed Nockerman. Rotunda hadn't seen her, so there was no eyewitness. Why mention it? But I believed him. And I had a damn good idea who he had heard arguing with Nocky that night.

Yet I said nothing. It was not the first time I had withheld from the authorities what might be crucial information in a capital crime, though I didn't make a habit of it. But if I was subpoenaed to testify in court, or before a grand jury, I'd have to talk; I never lied under oath.

And I didn't think Rotunda was lying about the woman. I knew, of course, that he lied when he said he had nothing to do with the Angler, Osvald murders—I was convinced he ordered the hits. So I repeated what Teddy Lane had told me. But by omitting the woman from the story, I wouldn't have to say who I thought she might be—and for the moment, I wouldn't have to think about her.

The captain finally told me, "This goddamn thing's a real mess jurisdiction-wise. The feds, Chicago, Lake County, everybody's gonna want a piece of this thing. Meanwhile, I got it, but it'll be one helluva fight to keep it. I guess you can go now, Mr. Wolf. But we'll have to talk to you again at greater length. I'll have one of my men drive you to Chicago."

Back at my apartment I telephoned Tina.

"Frank, I've been terribly worried," she said. "Where have you been? What happened?"

"I'll see you tonight and tell you the whole story."

"Are you all right?"

"Fine, but a little shaky."

"I love you," she said.

"Do you? I wonder." I had my doubts now.

She sent me a juicy kiss over the phone.

I had a couple of shots of Jack Daniel's after I hung up. Then I took a quick shower, shaved, and went to see Duffy.

I had always been honest with Duffy before. That's one of the reasons we got along, despite our long-term chronic feuding. Cops, reporters, and P.I.'s usually know when you're lying. So I had the impression throughout our conversation that Duffy knew I wasn't telling him everything. He was right, of course; I told him only what I wanted him to know, and I edited out the part about the woman again, as I had with the Lake County Sheriff.

Duffy was pleased and pissed. He was glad to have what looked like a lock on the murders—assuming that Lane would testify for the prosecution to save himself, which was a damn good bet. But Duffy was not too happy about my methods.

"You broke the law here, Wolf. How's that gonna help us put away Rotunda? I got nothing that's admissible in court. Besides, I got a duty to take you down for breaking and entering."

"You going to bust me?"

"I've got an obligation, Wolf. Your license is on the line here, maybe some time and a fine too. You know that, don't you?"

"Yeah, I know it."

"What did the Lake County Sheriff's people say about your breaking into Watt's place?"

"I neglected to mention it. Maybe you can do likewise."

"You asking me to withhold evidence?"

"No, just leave out the dull parts."

"Like you're doing to me right now. I know you're not telling me the whole story. I got a sixth sense for that."

I said nothing. Duffy leaned back and sighed. I caught a whiff of Tullamore Dew on his breath.

"Look, Wolf, you can explain how you made this case without saying you broke into Watt's apartment. But I don't like that, it's not your style."

"You telling me you never bent the law out of shape a little? Come on, Duffy, all you guys do it."

"Okay, for the sake of argument, suppose your story stands up to the State's Attorney here. You still got to do it all over again for the feds, and maybe to a Federal grand jury. What if there's a little discrepancy in your story? Or they get wise that you left something out? You know what the rap is for perjury? Or for concealing evidence?"

"Sure I do, Pat." I looked into Duffy's red, white, and blue eyes. "But who's going to accuse me?"

"When the time comes, we'll talk about it," he said. "So far you haven't lied under oath. All I got on you is your voluntary confession to a B and E. Although I didn't read you your Miranda. Meanwhile, I'm not sure I understand the mechanics of Nockerman's laundering operation."

"Ask your financial investigations people to explain it. And take a look at a guy named Lippert. He just started working for Lane at the brokerage firm. He smells kinda funny."

"You don't bring 'em in too neat," Duffy said. "Look at all the loose ends here. How deep is Mrs. Nockerman involved in the dope business? Who heisted Nockerman's money, if there was any money? Osvald's kinky bank. Lane's bullshit story about Nocky blowing away those South Americans. Jesus Christ, Wolf, there's loose strings all over the goddamn place."

"Look, Duffy," I said. "I'm laying the whole thing out for you on a silver platter. You got Watt, a professional hit man, the guy who probably killed Nockerman and the others. You got the why of it too."

"Watt is dead. I got no proof he killed anyone."

"But you got Rotunda, the coke dealer, the guy who hired Watt to waste everyone. You also got a multimillion-dollar dirty-money wash and some of the people who ran it. And you can tell your arson people that Watt torched Angler's garage. If that's not neat, what is? This is real life, Duffy."

"You say the sheriff's got Watt's .45?"

"Yeah, that's probably the murder weapon."

"Who owned it?"

"Sheriff says it's unregistered. What else you need?"

"Why the hell did Nockerman get wrapped up in this dope shit?" Duffy asked. "Didn't he have enough goddamn money?"

"He played for the action, not for the money."

"You think so?" Duffy asked. "I don't know, greed is something you never shake, like alcoholism. By the way, that Nockerman girl's a beauty."

"Look, Pat, this break-in thing could put me out of business. I'd like you to help me."

"Frank, why do you put me in this position?" He seemed genuinely sorry.

"I didn't have to tell you, did I? Besides, who was hurt?"

"I took an oath to uphold the law," Duffy said. "Goddamnit, Frank, why the hell did you tell me?"

"Confession is good for the soul."

"I'm no priest."

"You're no saint either."

"What the hell am I going to do about you?"

"Think about it for a while," I said. "A long while."

Duffy groaned, then he smiled. "I like you, Frank, but I don't trust you anymore. All right, I'll give it some thought."

47

I felt bad about losing Duffy's trust. He was a decent man and he always treated me as fairly as his job permitted. I knew I was beginning to slide and I didn't like the feeling. If I didn't grab something solid, I was afraid I'd fall all the way. I could buy my way back, if I had the inclination, but it might cost me more than I was willing to pay.

And I still owed Freedo. But I wasn't worried. I'd pay him eventually, I always do. But he'd have to wait, and so he'd no doubt send his Beast after me to help speed up my payments. No matter. I could handle it. I've always handled it. And I felt my luck was coming back—at least I was alive and healthy. Symmetry enough for anyone. But there was still a final hand to be played: Tina.

I had dinner with Tina that night at her apartment in the Hancock. When she opened the door to let me in I saw the ice crystals in her eyes; she was high. I said nothing.

I brought her up-to-date on most of what had happened since I last saw her, and as I finished my dessert while Tina still picked at her salad, I said, "I had to tell the cops about your mother. That she's hiding out in Palm Springs, and that she and your father were in the dope business together."

"You told the police about my mother? Was that absolutely necessary, Frank?" She was not as angry or upset as I thought she'd be.

"Teddy Lane's going to tell them too. He's going to testify

for the government in this thing and go into the Witness Protection Program."

"Will Mother go to jail?"

"Maybe not, if she gets a good lawyer. Depends how deep she was in."

After dinner we sat in Tina's living room side by side on the couch drinking coffee and Courvoisier, surrounded by photographs of her beloved daddy. I dreaded what I had to do next, but it had to be done. I took a deep breath and said, "Teddy told me your father killed a man."

She looked at me for a long moment, blinking. At last she said, "I don't believe it."

I recapped Lane's story about the dope deal off the Florida coast. When I had finished, she calmly took a sip of brandy, apparently not shocked or even surprised. Then she glanced away, looking from photo to photo of her father, her eyes misting. Finally, she turned back to me.

"No," she said. "Teddy did it. He's the one who killed that man on the boat. He just wants to blame Daddy for it. My father couldn't do a thing like that. He was a sweet, gentle man."

"There's no reason for Lane to lie," I said. "Too much time has passed. The case has been closed for years: accidental death by drowning. Where's the advantage for Lane in lying?"

She didn't answer.

I took another deep breath and stood up, hands in pockets, and looked down at Tina. Then I repeated the story Rotunda had told me about hearing a woman come into Nockerman's apartment that night and kill him. She listened raptly, seeming to ponder the meaning of every detail. When I finished there was a long silence. At last, as if she had been mentally working through a complex mathematical problem, she whispered her answer: "Rita."

"No," I said.

She seemed puzzled. "Mother?"

"No, not your mother."

"Then who?"

"It was you, Tina."

She blanched. "What are you saying, Frank?"

I told her, slowly and calmly. "You killed your father. I don't know why. Maybe you'll tell me."

"Are you insane, for God's sake?"

"Only you and Jimmy had a key to his apartment. And Jimmy was out of town."

"No," she said. "Rita must've also had a key."

I went on. "You let yourself into the apartment. Your father was in the study. You went in. You argued about something. Money, maybe. Then you shot him."

"That's bullshit," she shrieked.

"You shot him, and you got the hell out. Later you remembered that in your haste to leave you'd forgotten the gun. So you went back. You discovered that the gun was gone. The briefcase full of money was gone too. You panicked. The missing murder weapon had your prints on it. And whoever took the gun also grabbed the money. As it turned out, the people who took the gun used it to kill a couple of their associates. They were all in the dope business together, including your father.

"So you cooked up that story you told the cops—and your mother, and me. You figured eventually the police—or me, after I came into it—would find out that your father was dealing coke. We'd write off the killing as a drug murder, which it might've been if you hadn't walked in. That's why you kept insisting a briefcase full of money had been taken. You were sure of it. But how did you know? Because you saw it that night. And when you came back later to get the gun, you didn't see it."

"That's crazy, Frank. This South American—what's his name? He killed Daddy. Then he makes up a story about hearing a woman come in and firing a shot."

"If Rotunda had been there first and killed your father, the money would've been gone by the time you came in. So, of course, you wouldn't have known it was taken."

She looked at me, frowning, bewildered. Then she smiled.

"You're mistaken, Frank. Rotunda killed Daddy. He heard me come in and ran into the adjacent room."

"But you told me you stayed with your father's body all night. You stayed till dawn, you told me. Then you called the cops. How'd Rotunda and his people leave without your seeing them?"

"I must've dozed off."

"I'm sorry, Tina. I don't believe you. Now tell me what really happened. I'll try to help you."

"You don't believe me? Why? Because what that South American told you? He's a goddamn criminal. A pathological liar."

"Yeah, but in this case I believe him," I said. "I wish I didn't, but I do. For a long time, Tina, I had a hunch about you. I kept ignoring it, but it wouldn't go away. Turns out my hunch was right."

"I don't know what you're talking about, Frank."

"Why'd you kill your father, Tina?"

"I didn't kill him."

"Where was the gun that night? On the desk, or in it?"

"I didn't do it, Frank. I loved him. I swear to God."

"You kissed your father that night."

"Of course. So what?"

"Rotunda said it was not a daughter's kiss."

"Excuse me? What are you saying?"

"It was not a daughter's kiss," I repeated.

"Jesus Christ, Frank, can't you see what this Rotunda bastard's trying to do? First of all, he's trying to make it so you don't trust me. Then he lays out this bullshit so that I'll be charged with Daddy's murder."

"But he didn't know it was you who came in that night."

I leaned over, grabbed her by the shoulders and yanked her violently to her feet. We were face-to-face, breathing on one another. Her usually fragrant breath was sour. "Your father was a coke dealer, a killer, and God knows what else. What else was he, Tina?"

"Let me go." She struggled to free herself.

"You were lovers, weren't you? You and your father."

"No," she screamed.

"Yes, Tina."

She shuddered, threw her hands over her ears. "I don't want to hear this, Frank. *Please.*"

I said it again. "You were lovers." But I wanted her to tell me *no*, they weren't. I wanted her to swear Rotunda was a liar, or to give me some convincing explanation for what he thought he had heard that night.

But in a whisper then she said, "Yes."

And that look I knew so well in all its endless varieties came over her face: the confession of guilt and the profound relief that follows. I released my grip on her and she fell sobbing to the couch.

I picked up one of the many framed photos of Nockerman from an end table and examined it briefly. He had the same expression in his eyes that you see in the self-portraits of Van Gogh. And sometimes in the eyes of gamblers who throw their lives away on impossible long shots.

I smashed the photograph against the table. Tina flinched. Then, as if I were swinging a sickle, I swept away the entire gallery of Nockerman photographs from the table top. They flew like missiles across the room and crashed noisily to the floor.

I turned back to Tina. She was curled up on the couch and cowering, as if she were waiting for me to start on her. I sat down and picked up both of her hands in mine.

"Tell me, Tina."

She shook her head, sobbing quietly. I embraced her, patting her gently on the back as if I were trying to becalm a frightened infant awakened in the night.

She spoke in a tremulous, childlike voice. "He raped me. When I was sixteen. He came to my room one night. Maybe it wasn't really rape. Maybe it was my fault. Maybe I was too seductive. I don't know. I was an adopted child, lonely, unhappy, confused, very unsure of myself. My mother was giving me hell in those days. Picking on me for everything. She was on Daddy's case too. He came to me that night and said he just wanted to hold me.

"Maybe I should've resisted more. I should never have let it get started. Once it began, I didn't have the power to stop it. He told me it wasn't wrong because we weren't related by blood. I should've told the cops, my mother, someone. But I didn't. So I suppose it's my fault. But I loved him. And I hated him too. And God, how I hated myself. Maybe I should have told someone, but I was so ashamed, I couldn't face anyone. It went on even after they got divorced. But then, just a few weeks after I was twenty, I told him no more, it was over. And it was. But he never gave up trying. He told me I was the only thing on the face of this earth that he ever truly loved. He said he loved me from the moment he saw me as a child. I wish to God he had never started this."

"That bastard," I said. "But I sensed it. Weeks ago. I had a hunch. Nothing concrete. Just a feeling. But I told myself:

no, it's too ugly. So I stopped thinking about it. Then Rotunda told me what happened the night you shot your father and I put it together. Not the whole picture, but part of it anyway. And I still didn't believe it. Not entirely. Until you told me. . . ."

I was silent for a moment.

Then I said, "Okay, babe, don't worry. I'm going to help you. You should've told me about this in the beginning. It would've been easier. I understand now why you killed him. He deserved it. Problem is, a jury may not see it that way."

"That's not why I killed him. I mean, I didn't kill him for any specific reason. It was an accident."

"Why'd you go to his apartment that night?"

"Because I was out of coke and out of cash. And he always had plenty of both around."

"What did you and he argue about?"

"He wanted me to go away with him to Barbados. He wanted us to live there together. He said he would soon close the biggest business deal of his life and he'd have millions. We could live together like royalty, he said, and the rest of the world could go to hell. He always talked crazy like that when he was stoned. I knew he was high when I came in. I gave him a kiss, just a peck to say hello, but he grabbed me and kissed me back hard."

"Why would he do that with people in the next room?"

"Daddy didn't give a damn about what anyone thought. Not when he was loaded. Coke does strange things to people."

"Did you know there were people in the apartment?"

"No."

"What happened after he kissed you?"

"He started insisting that I go away with him. I told him he was insane. He got angry at me. He yelled at me, threatened to tell my mother about us, threatened to dissolve my trust fund so that I wouldn't get any money. Then he turned away from me in his chair. I said to him he sometimes got me so angry I could kill him. You know how people say that. They don't mean it. But there was a big gun on Daddy's desk and I picked it up and put it against the back of his head. I swear to God, I had no intention of using it. Then it went off. It was an accident, I swear to you, Frank."

I didn't know if I believed her.

She went on. "Daddy slumped over his desk, then fell from his chair to the floor. I was horrified. I dropped the gun and just stood there. I don't know how long, but it seemed like hours. Then suddenly I got sick. I got the shakes. I panicked. I had to get out of there. I don't even remember riding down in the elevator. I got in the car and just drove. I was dazed.

"Hours later my brain cleared and I discovered myself parked at some deserted beach. I didn't even know where. As it turned out I was way up north somewhere, past Lake Forest. Then I remembered I had left the gun at Daddy's. I went back to the apartment. The gun was gone, and so was the money. I tried to figure out what happened, how someone got into the apartment. I couldn't come up with a reasonable explanation. It never occurred to me that people might've been there when I came in. I thought I might be a suspect in Daddy's killing. Later, I figured it was the dope dealers Daddy did business with who had been there. I was sure it was them; anyone might've taken the money, but who else would've taken the gun? Anyway, I stayed with Daddy for the rest of the night, and when it was daylight I called the police."

"Does your mother know you killed him?"

"No."

"If it was an accident, why didn't you tell the cops?"

"I was afraid then, and I'm still afraid. I don't want to go to prison, Frank. You've got to help me."

"I'll do everything I can."

"No. Don't do anything. And don't say anything."

"Meaning what?"

"Only you know I killed Daddy, Frank. And only you understand why. I don't see that it's necessary for you to tell the police. They'll think these dope dealers murdered him and that'll be the end of it."

I stood up and walked around the living room, feeling the lush carpet beneath my feet, soft and silent like a well-kept putting green. I reflected on the past few months, looked back on it all then through a different lens. There were distortions in the picture and it was out of focus.

I wondered if Tina had used me as a hedge. Maybe she had made a longshot bet that I'd fall in love with her. Then, if I discovered that she murdered her father, maybe she'd have had my love as her insurance against my taking what I knew to the cops. And maybe I'd help her blow some smoke here and there to cloud things up a little. Maybe that's why it had all seemed so easy, and why she got so involved with me so quickly—or appeared to, anyway. If that was how she played it, she lost. Because what I felt for her, though more intense than affection, could not be called love.

"Tomorrow," I said, "first thing in the morning, I'm going to call a friend of mine. He's one of the best criminal lawyers in Chicago."

"No, Frank." She shook her head wildly.

"Then you and I will go to his office together and you'll tell him everything. From the beginning."

"I have no intention of going to prison—"

I interrupted her. "When you've finished telling the lawyer, we'll go to the police, you, me, and the lawyer, and you'll give yourself up to another friend of mine, a Captain Duffy."

"Like hell I will."

"You'll work out a solid defense," I said. "There are mitigating circumstances. A good lawyer will figure some angle."

"No, Frank. They'll send me to prison."

"I'll also get you some first-rate professional help. For your drug problem. And counseling for what happened with your . . ."

I was going to say *father,* but the word stuck in my craw, it didn't seem appropriate. So I didn't finish the sentence.

"I can't face all that, Frank," she said calmly.

She stood, and from somewhere—maybe from beneath a cushion of the couch—she had pulled a gun. It looked like a small-caliber automatic, but I couldn't see it clearly from across the room.

"What are you going to do, Tina, kill me?"

She pointed the gun at my mid-section.

"There's something else I've got to get off my conscience, Frank."

"What?"

"You know those two men who talked to you?"

"Which two men?"

"The ones who asked you to drop the case."

"The ones who beat the shit out of me and broke my foot?"

"I didn't want them to hurt you, Frank. I only told them to talk you out of it."

"How? By force of logic? Jesus Christ, Tina. Why?"

"You know why. Because I was afraid you'd find out the truth about me. I'm sorry, Frank, but I'm not going to jail."

She extended her arm, aiming the gun, finger tightening on the trigger. We looked at each other for a long time without saying a word. I waited for the shot, my stomach contracting in expectation. Then her concentration broke, and she raised the gun to her head.

"Don't," I said. "Please, Tina. I'm going to help you." I walked slowly toward her, my eyes fixed on hers. I reached up carefully, hardly breathing, and wrapped my hand around her hand.

I was taking the gun away from her when she pulled the trigger. One of the tall windows that gave on the city exploded into countless shards. She fell to the floor, weeping.

I reached down to lift her. I wanted to hold her in my arms like a child and comfort her. But she twisted away.

"Leave me alone, Frank."

I put the gun in my pocket, turned, and walked slowly across the room to the shattered window. The wind gushed in from the lake, a sound like the roaring of the trading pits heard from a great distance.

I thought about Nockerman and how I had once admired him. I felt nothing for him now but a cold, chronic rage. I thought about Tina, and how I had not really known her until tonight. And I thought about myself, what I was and what I had become, and about who and what had worked the changes in me.

I looked down at the city far below. The lights blinked and flashed, moved and crisscrossed incessantly, a video game gone manic. And everybody plays, whether they want to or not. I guess you might say it's an addiction and an obsession, like cocaine, or gambling, or a voracious need for love, or an insatiable appetite for sex or its perversions, or a lust for money, or for power, or whatever it is you can't get enough of. And what's enough of anything if you're obsessed by it? When it kills you, that's enough.

epilogue

About a month later the news broke. The story hit front pages around the country and made all the network newscasts.

The FBI had been running an undercover sting op here at the futures exchanges, the Mercantile and the Board of Trade. For two years the good, gray moles of Uncle Sam impersonated fast-buck pit traders, buying and selling commodities. They hung out with coke dealers and flakes, they got cozy with the scam artists who screwed their customers, prearranged their trades, did business outside the pits in violation of the rules. They lived the lavish lifestyle, threw money around like confetti. It must have been great fun, one of those dream assignments that later become the stuff of legend.

Then they went public, presented evidence to a federal grand jury, the indictments came back, and the feds went to trial armed to the toenails with tapes, photos, documents, eyewitness corroboration, everything needed to cinch their cases.

A lot of people were hurt. And some even got what they deserved. You could call it cosmic equity if you believed in that kind of bookkeeping. They tell us it's all cleaned up now and it's going to stay that way. Maybe. But I always bet on human nature. And when I do, I never lose.

Marc Davis is a former commodities broker whose experiences on the Chicago Board of Trade have contributed to the background authenticity of *Dirty Money*. The author of one previous novel, he lives with his family near Chicago.